THE MASTER CAT

The True and Unexpurgated Story of

PUSS IN BOOTS

by

David Garnett

with illustrations by
Nerissa Garnett

SBN 333 17837 8

First published 1974 by
MACMILLAN LONDON LIMITED
London and Basingstoke
Associated companies in New York Dublin
Melbourne Johannesburg & Delhi

Printed in Great Britain by
W & J MACKAY LIMITED, CHATHAM

TO

Henrietta Partridge

CONTENTS

Part One

Part One

CHAPTER ONE

Christopher inherits no ordinary cat

THERE was a miller who had three sons. The mill was large and stood on a hill, and the miller was a rich man because all the farmers brought him their corn to grind and all the bakers came to him to buy his flour. Most mills have dirty corners with spilt grain, and above the creaking of the mill's sails and the whistling wind you can often hear the squeaking of mice and the scurrying feet of rats. But no rat dared enter the miller's granary, and no baker had ever come to complain of mouse-droppings in a sack of flour coming from that mill. This was because of the miller's cat, the largest and handsomest fellow ever seen in the Kingdom of Northumberland.

One day the old miller and his three sons were hoisting sacks of wheat into the granary. Wheat sacks were heavier in those days than they are now and held ten quarters of wheat: two hundredweight and a half; so it needed a strong man to carry one on his back, and a man like Hercules to lift one off the ground.

But though the miller's sons were all strong men, they were not lifting the sacks. They had a pulley fixed to a beam that stuck out from the roof of the granary, with a chain running through the pulley and a shiny steel ring at the end of the chain.

The second son, James, standing in the waggon full of sacks of wheat, pulled the chain through the steel ring and pushed one corner of a sack through the loop he had made. Then the youngest son pulled the other end of the chain, the noose tightened and the sack rose up out of the waggon, spinning and dangling in the air until it was hoisted just above the level of the granary floor, where the eldest son, John, was standing. John caught hold of the sack and pulled it in, Christopher lowered it, then John pulled the noose loose, and while the chain rattled down again and was fastened to another sack, John put his arms round the sack to lift it a bit and pushing with his knees, shoved it into position beside the row of sacks in the granary. Later on, when there was a wind, and the sails were turning, they would move the sack to the wooden chute, untie its mouth and empty a stream of pale gold grain to where it was fed between the great millstones which would grind it into flour. But the wind wasn't blowing that day, and they were getting the sacks of grain ready for the next time when it did.

They had hoisted up about three-quarters of the sacks in the waggon when the old miller came out and stood watching. Then he stepped under the sack that was swinging high up nearly level with the granary floor. Suddenly the corner of the sack tore, the lug slipped through the noose of chain, and the heavy sack of wheat fell on top of the old man, knocking him down, and while he lay there a stream of wheat, pouring from the torn corner of the sack, built up into a little mound beside his silver white hair and his red face.

'Well, Father's got his full measure there,' said John looking down from the granary floor.

'Yes, that one has flattened him,' said James climbing out of the waggon in which he was standing.

'It's not often that the lug of a sack tears like that,' said Christopher. John came down the ladder from the granary loft and the three sons stood looking at the fallen sack. Then Christopher pulled a length of chain through the steel ring, slipped the loop round the other corner of the sack and hauled it, now only partly full, up off his father. But the miller still lay flat on the ground without moving, while the half-empty sack swung and twirled in the air above him. He just lay there watching it with his blue eyes open, but saying nothing.

Then John and James lifted the body of their father and carried him into the millhouse and up to his bed and Christopher followed as soon as he had lowered the dangling sack of wheat to the ground.

'I shall have to shovel up that spilt grain and see that no dirt goes in with it when I fill the sack up,' he was thinking when he went into his father's bedroom.

The old man lay there groaning and fetching his breath, with his boots and his gaiters stretched out on the patchwork quilt. At last he began to speak, but in a whisper, and his sons had to lean over him with their floury heads knocking together to catch his words.

'I am dying,' he said, 'and you will inherit all I have. To John I leave the mill, the millhouse and the milling business. To James, my second son, I leave my train of pack-horses. There is a good carrier's trade to be had nowadays with the upland sheep farmers, for the price of wool is high. To my youngest son, Christopher . . .' But just then a breeze springing up set the sails of the mill turning and creaking, and Christopher missed his father's words.

The old man lay there silent, and his three sons stood waiting, but their father only groaned. At last Christopher asked: 'And what am I to have, father?'

'I told ye, but I'll say it again: Christopher must have the cat.' It was all John and James could do to keep from laughing, while poor Christopher stood at first dumb with dismay.

At last he exclaimed: 'Say that again father. I don't understand.' But the old miller did not speak again, although Christopher went on arguing with him. At last John told him plainly that their father was dead and pushed him out of the bedroom.

The funeral was much like other funerals, and after it there was a supper for all the farmers and their wives who had come to see the old man buried.

There was barley wine, saddle of mutton with rowan jelly, turnips mashed in butter, new peas and then cheesecakes and a blackberry and apple pie and Cotherstone cheese with a nip of sloe gin.

Next morning John went to the mill and called out to Harry, the hired hand: 'I am now the master here; you must do my bidding, fellow, and work for me.'

James went to the stable and called out to the stable boy:

'I am now the master here. You must do my bidding, boy, and work for me.'

Harry only scowled and nodded at John, for he did not like being called 'fellow', but the boy, Bob, pulled his forelock and said: 'Yes, Measter Jim.'

But Christopher went sadly into the parlour and there he found the big tom cat lying asleep upon a cushion in the best armchair. He had eaten and drunk his fill after the miller's funeral, and he was sleeping it off. If there had been a rat, now would have been his chance to slip into the granary, but there wasn't a rat or a mouse within half a mile.

'Puss,' said Christopher waking him up, 'Puss, I have come

to claim you, for it seems that you are all the goods that I have in the world, and I must set out today to seek my fortune, as I have no mind to work without wages for my brother John, who will prove a hard master. A cat is a useless sort of thing at best, and you cannot be of much service to me. I could have a pair of gloves made out of your skin, and they might sell for a crown when the weather turns colder.'

Puss opened his mouth and yawned, and Christopher looked at his pink tongue arching between his gleaming white teeth. Then Puss stretched out each of his legs in turn and sank his sharp claws into the cushion.

'In Godmanchester the youngest son comes by all,' said Christopher. 'If only father had had his mill there I should be a rich man, and my two brothers would have only your skin to share between them to keep them from the cold.'

'Not so much about my skin, if you please,' said Puss. 'Such jokes come badly from an old friend. If you think that all the service I can do you is to keep your hands warm, you are mistaken. I am worth ten thousand times more than a pair of gloves, or even a muff. If you do not think so you can skin me, and welcome. I am serious when I say this.'

When Christopher heard the cat speak he was overcome by astonishment. But the morose tone of voice in which Puss spoke and the way in which he kept yawning, showing all his sharp teeth and stretching out his claws, made Christopher think it was best to give him a civil answer; besides which, if Puss could talk, he was no ordinary cat and perhaps his words were true. So he said: 'Puss, I never thought to hear you speak, but you must not bear me a grudge for my idle words. You know I only spoke as I did because I do not know what to do, or where to turn for help. My brothers will turn me out of the house, and I have only half a guinea in the world.'

'That is why I think that your jokes are unseasonable,' said Puss. 'In an ordinary way I should have taken no notice, for I flatter myself that I have a very keen sense of humour. The mice, I think, will bear me out as to that.'

Christopher took hold of one of Pussy's paws, but awkwardly, for he was shy of a talking cat, and said, rather shamefaced: 'You and I are such old friends. Do not quarrel with me now that I am in such distress, but since you can speak your mind, advise me what I had best do, and then I shall see that you have found your tongue to some purpose.'

Puss was silent, and Christopher went on: 'I am a poor boy and I must make my way in the world, but to tell the truth I have no notion how to set about it.'

'Many men have made a great figure in the world with nothing more than you have got now when they set out. Did you never hear the story of a young fellow, a few years back, called Dick? And he was nothing like so good-looking as you are. In fact my friendship and your good looks are all you have in the world.'

Christopher said nothing. He was staring into the fire and thinking, for the first time in his life, of the future, an exercise which made him unhappy, as he could see nothing but a long, long road with nothing at the end of it, and with nothing to eat or to drink by the way. Not even blackberries in the hedges.

Taking Christopher's silence for consent, Puss began the story of Dick as follows.

CHAPTER TWO

How Dick was saved from slavery and made a rich man

'Not many years since, when our English ships were roving everywhere, sometimes trading with Spain and to the Middle Sea, and sometimes harrying the Irish Saints, the Captain of a longship put in at Galway where he bought a cargo of Irish boys and girls to carry as slaves to Constantinople, the Western World's market for such merchandise.

'One of the boys was singled out directly he went aboard, not for his good looks, nor for his fine raiment, nor for the whiteness of his skin, for he was the ugliest, dirtiest boy among them, dressed in rags, with scurf in his hair, a cast in one eye and a lean wizened face as though he had been put out to nurse with a nanny goat.

'What distinguished him was that he spoke English and not Erse, and that he carried a fine, well-grown tortoiseshell cat in his arms. When the Captain first saw this boy, he swore he would throw him overboard to save ship's biscuit, for no Byzantine lady would wish to have such a misshapen goaty creature near her; but afterwards, seeing that the crew were kind to the lad for the cat's sake, he made the best of a bad bargain by ordering him to be the ship's boy thereafter. Thus, owing to his cat, the second day out, the lad's chains were struck off and he was given his freedom.

'The ship had a quiet passage across the Bay of Biscay and round the coast of Portugal and Spain, but as soon as she had passed the straits, she ran into a northerly gale. Try how he would, the Captain was driven in to the shores of Africa. At last there was nothing for it but to anchor and lie up until the storm abated. A week went by and still the wind howled round them, coming in blasts that would have torn the sails out of any ship, and it was a wonder that the bare mast was not uprooted. Still the sea ran mountains high and kept them all baling. When a big sea broke over them all hands were at work to lighten her before the next breaker came along and swamped her. The Captain then, for lack of a dipper, pulled off his steel morion to scoop up the salt water and work with the crew to keep the ship afloat.

'Provisions failed them, and there was still no sign of a break in the weather, so in the end the Captain ordered them to slip the cable and beach the ship. But first he had the chains and manacles taken off his cargo of slave boys and girls so as to give those that could swim a chance of saving their lives. Besides he may have hoped to treat with the Moors and sell the lads and lasses in a Saracen slave market if he could not reach the one in Byzantium.

'A giant wave carried the ship right up the beach and they landed safely and what was as wonderful was that they were kindly received. But they soon found that the Moors were but little better off for food than they were themselves.

'Africa, they said, was overrun with vermin, and such was

the plague that the rats and mice devoured the corn in the fields before it was harvested and even climbed the palm trees and ate up the dates before they ripened. All the food they had came by ship from their friends the Moors in Spain. However, seeing that the Captain had a cargo of slave boys and girls, the Moors took them at once to their Bashaw, the famous Mullisheg, a tall hungry-looking man with hollow cheeks under his black beard, sorrowful eyes and twitching fingers.

'"Before we buy or sell," said the Captain, "I must beg you for something with which to stay the stomachs of my men, for it is three days since we finished our last biscuit, and the slave boys and girls are so weak for want of food that they can scarcely stand on their feet."

'Mullisheg somewhat sorrowfully invited the Captain and some of the crew into his palace. They had time to look about in wonder at the rich carpets hanging on the walls and the brass lamps hanging from the ceiling before the Moorish slaves brought in a roasted kid and many fine dishes of sweetmeats. The sailors' mouths watered at the smell of the roast kid and the gravy, and Mullisheg was just bidding the Captain to help himself, when before the words were out of his mouth, a whole multitude of rats and mice rushed out from all sides and carried off every scrap of food.

'"They are worse than ever before," said Mullisheg, making what excuses he could. "They are a very great inconvenience, but I beg you to believe that they are not always as bad as they have been today. Usually they only take the best bits and we are able to stay our hunger with what they have left behind." Then he ordered his slaves to bring whatever was left in the larder. Luckily there was a large dish of boiled rice and a lot of Spanish onions, which the company greedily devoured.

'"What you want is a good cat," said one of the sailors. But after a few questions it came out that the Bashaw did not understand what the sailor had said, for he had never seen a cat and had no knowledge of our race. I have my own ideas of why he was so ignorant, which I will explain later.

'Well, all the Englishmen were astonished by this, then they recollected that the ugly cabin boy had a fine cat and at once sent word to him to bring her in to show the Bashaw what a cat was. When she was set down Pussy did not waste time in letting herself be admired, but instantly began hunting out the rats and the mice too, and so diligently did she pursue them that in an hour's time she had caught and killed fifty or sixty. It was quick work you may think, but then the rats knew no more about cats than the Bashaw himself.

'Never having seen a cat before you can imagine how Mullisheg was overcome by her grace and beauty. And when he found that she was as useful as she was handsome, he fell down on his face and returned thanks to Allah who had taken compassion on him and his people, for he was persuaded that Puss was sent from Heaven. The next thing was that he must buy her. Dick declared that he would take nothing less than ten pieces of gold, which was the greatest sum he could think of, but Mullisheg gave him five hundred; and to reward the Captain he bought his whole cargo of Irish slaves at a price greatly above their true worth. Very soon the Palace and the kitchens were clear of vermin. Puss had a fine family of kittens who carried on her work, and in a couple of years the plague was over and rats and mice became almost as unknown as cats had been before.'

'But how came it that cats, the most necessary of man's companions, were unknown in the Kingdom of Morocco?' asked Christopher.

'I think that this is the reason,' replied Puss. 'I cannot swear that I am right, for it is my own idea, and it has not been proved. In ancient times the Egyptians, who were the wisest of peoples, believed that the cat was sacred. They worshipped their cats, treated them like gods and goddesses while they were alive, and after their deaths made mummies of them to keep Pharaoh company in his pyramid. Well, after the false prophet Mohamed set the Arabs rampaging about the world, they conquered the Egyptians and overset their idols and killed all the sacred cats. And from Egypt they soon spread over North Africa and into Spain, exterminating all the cats as they went. All that had come to pass long before Mullisheg was born, and so it was that there was not a cat in Morocco except perhaps for a few wild ones in the Atlas Mountains. That is my explanation, which you might as well accept until you can think of a better.'

'But what happened to Dick after he had sold his cat for such a fortune?'

'Dick continued with the English Captain for some years. He was made ship's purser. Later he left the sea and became a merchant in the City of London, where he grew so rich that he was made Lord Mayor three times before he died. But for his having a cat, he would have lived and died a slave, and being so ugly he would have been likely to have got a double share of the lash.'

CHAPTER THREE

Puss needs to cut a good figure in the world

'WHY did you tell me that story?' asked Christopher when Puss had finished. 'Was it to raise me up to hope for impossibilities? I know you are a fine cat, but nobody would pay five pounds for you, let alone five hundred.'

'First you wanted to sell my skin—now you are hoping to sell me,' said Puss in a morose tone of voice.

'I know that you are as good a cat as ever that young fellow Dick had, but nowadays Morocco has all the cats it wants. Besides it is a thousand miles from here.'

At these words Puss smiled at the simplicity of his master and exclaimed: 'Morocco! The only kind of Morocco we want is of a different sort. Nothing more than a pair of high boots made of morocco leather, so that I can go about the world cutting a good figure.'

'What do you mean by that?' asked Christopher. 'I cannot

understand what you are saying. Why should a cat like you want boots?'

'Why, if you were to get me a pair of red morocco leather boots,' answered Puss, 'then I should be able to do much more for you than ever that tortoiseshell Queen did for Dick. But I must be able to go among strangers and get myself respected. The best schemes will miscarry unless one can make a good figure in the world.'

Just then Christopher looked out of the window and saw the shoemaker passing by. The man was saddler as well as shoemaker and had come about putting a leather patch on one of the pack-saddles of James's ponies, which is how he came to be up at the millhouse just at that time. So Christopher put his head out of the window and called out after him. The shoemaker turned back, and when the miller's son told him that he wanted a pair of red morocco leather boots made for his cat, he took out his measuring stick and went down on one knee in front of the chair where Puss was sitting, as though the request were the most ordinary one in the world. Christopher said they were to be of the finest quality and that he wanted them done as soon as possible.

Next day the shoemaker came back with the boots, for he had sat up all night sewing them. It was a job after his own heart, and the pony's pack-saddle could wait. He had never made boots for a cat before, and had never heard tell of any other shoemaker making them.

Puss stretched out his legs and with some little difficulty got into the boots, the shoemaker asking him several times to keep his claws in. Once they had been pulled up his furry legs, the top-boots were seen to be of the smartest cut, more suitable in style for an officer in the Life Guards than for any cat.

Puss stamped his feet once or twice and then began to swagger about in military fashion and twirl his whiskers; then he went and studied his appearance in a long glass that stood in one corner of the room. The shoemaker stood watching him, lost in admiration of his own work. And Christopher was paying him with his last half-guinea, as his brothers John and James came into the room.

Seeing Puss standing up and looking at himself in the glass they gave loud guffaws, and then seeing their young brother taking the last of his money out of his purse, they laughed louder still at his simplicity.

'A fine fool you are, Kit,' said John, 'to be throwing away your last penny on a cat that will soon take to his heels and carry off the boots with him. Nobody with any sense would think of having boots made for a cat.'

Then both the brothers abused him and declared they would do nothing more for such a wastrel, and John ended by telling him that he and his cat must be off within the hour.

Puss did not care to listen to such harsh words and, after spitting in one corner of the room to show his anger and contempt, he left the house. But before he departed with his young master he took the old miller's stick in his paw and an empty sack from the granary—a small one such as they use for clover seed. He threw it over his shoulder, for he well knew what he was about.

But Christopher went into the kitchen where Emily, who cooked and did all the housework in the mill and had nursed Christopher after his mother died, was waiting to kiss him goodbye. But she did not waste much time on kisses. She just said: 'I've put a bit in here to last you for a day or two on your journey. It's a crying shame; it is so. I spoke my mind to Master John and told him he could turn me away if he were so minded after I had been here forty years, but I would speak out.'

And she handed him a knapsack in which there was a loaf of brown bread, a packet of oatcakes, a big cut of cheese, a thick cut of ham, a pat of butter and a pot of bilberry jam.

'How shall I carry all this, Emily?' asked Christopher.

'It'll get lighter as you travel,' said Emily. 'Well, good luck to you. You do look a pair, to be sure. With those smart boots, I couldn't tell whether Puss were Master or Man.' And Emily pushed him out of the kitchen just before John came in, for he might be grudging the ham.

'This way, young master,' said Puss, pointing with his stick to the pony track which led from the corn lands where the mill stood on a hill to the upland pastures and the distant moors beyond.

'What, do you want to take me into Scotland? I will not follow you there, for the Scots are a devilish people who think nothing of burning an English farm, with the farmer's wife and her babies inside, when they come raiding into England,' said Christopher.

'No, we will keep south of the Border,' answered Puss. 'As for the Scots being a devilish people, they only do to the Northumberland men what is done to them. And if you were to count heads, I think we English, for I count myself an English cat, though there was a Wild Cat from Inverness among my ancestors, I think we English have the best of it, as we do of the Welsh and the Irish, not to go further afield to France and Spain. And nearer home, we North Country folk are each of us worth three of the silly men of Sussex.'

With such boastful words did Puss while away the hours while they trudged side by side into the hills. Fields and hedgerows fell away, hazel and oak being replaced by a rare mountain ash, and laid hedges by stone walls.

Presently they came down into a dale with a road winding up it beside a river full of shallows and sandbanks and salmon pools. They followed the road upstream, and when it grew dark they climbed up to a haybarn on the edge of the moor. The stone barn was full of newly swept up hay, and there they had their supper. Poor Christopher was aching in every limb. It was not his weary legs that made him begin to snuffle and cry, but the strangeness of everything since the death of his old father. He had loved the old man and had trusted him, and he had not only lost his only protector, but had been left to seek his fortune with nought but a cat—and such a strange kind of a cat too. He had known Puss from when he was a kitten, but who could have guessed that he could talk and lecture him about Ancient Egypt and Sacred Cats and that he should boast about a Wild Cat ancestor from Inverness?

Puss saw that his master was crying and pushed up against him in his rough way.

'Lie down in the hay, Master. If my plans go right you will never need to shed another tear.'

'I'm not crying, Puss. It's the hay dust makes my eyes water,' said Christopher between his sobs. Puss put his paws on Christopher's shoulders; then he pushed him backwards into the hay, curled up beside him and began purring. Soon Christopher was feeling better, and was almost dropping off to sleep when Puss said: 'When you wake up you will find me gone, and I may be away on your business for most of the day. You lie close here until I come back, and I expect to have some good news to tell you. For I have not brought you all this way without a purpose.' Then he stuck his claws into Christopher's jacket and began 'teasing tow' as they say, until he lay down again and began purring until Christopher had fallen asleep.

CHAPTER FOUR

Puss goes to Court and is well received

THE King of Northumberland was very partial to grouse.
Indeed there was no dish which he held comparable to a
roast grouse basted with the gravy from another, older bird.
All through the summer he counted the days to the twelfth
of August, and directly it was past he wanted no dish set
before him but only grouse. At breakfast he would eat a cold
bird left from the night before, and, as he was a great glutton,
he set down in his diary every day when he had eaten grouse;
and a day so marked was not counted as a day wasted.

Puss and Christopher had set out on the nineteenth of
August, but, like all of His Majesty's subjects, Puss knew that
the King had not tasted grouse that year. The weather had
been steamy with mists and fogs on the moors, and no one had
been able to bring down even a brace. In those days there were
no fowling pieces; the birds had either to be netted or knocked
over with a crossbow or a Venetian harquebus. That goes some

way to explain the poor success of the King's gamekeepers. Also it had been a warm early spring with a big snowfall at the end of May when the chicks were hatching out, so they were scarce. A third cause was a multitude of gypsies who had come that year, though where from no one could say. They had been roving the moors, and most of the coveys, misliking their company, had flown north across the Border into Scotland.

Like all cats who grow to a good size, Puss was a hardened poacher and knew as much about the coverts and game preserves of the Kingdom as anyone in it. Leaving Christopher asleep in the haybarn, he made his way uphill to a lonely piece of moorland called High Crag, at Ridley Stokoe, where his first care was to sit down and pull off his new boots, which he hid under a large tuft of heather.

Nothing can be achieved without patience, but this was a virtue of which Puss possessed a far greater stock than any ordinary sportsman. It was dark; it was foggy; not a star could be seen; but Puss went forward very cautiously, inch by inch, with the sack upon his shoulder, stopping every yard and listening to every sound, peering about on all sides in the dark, and sniffing every patch of heather. When he moved he was careful not to brush against the tall tufts of ling and never to set his pads where he might start a stone rolling. Puss knew that the grouse often came to High Crag to spend the night. Several times he smelt where the birds had been. At last dawn came: Puss was soaked with dew, drops of which ran down each of his whiskers; it was cold as it is always on the high moors at dawn. Puss could only see about twenty yards because of the mist, which as the sun rose began curling away into the hollows. Then Puss saw a sprig of heather shake and heard the note of a grouse. He knew that soon the birds would begin to move about and that they were very close.

Now though this story of Puss catching grouse takes a long time in the telling, it took longer in the doing. Puss was faint with excitement, but his brain was clear, and when it came to the actual catching of the birds, it went like a dream. First one bird came poking round the clump of heather where Puss lay hidden. Puss seized it by the throat, bit through the spine just below the head and thrust it into the sack. Then he waited, still as death, only the tip of his tail moving this way and that, and having to swallow the saliva in his mouth. Another bird came suddenly in reach and Puss pounced on him. In this way he got four of the young birds, but after that the others were suspicious and suddenly took wing.

Puss threw the sack over his shoulder, and as he was wet and stiff with the cold he began to run down the side of the crag; and it was not long till he got to the spot where he had laid his boots. He sat down to put them on, but found this was no easy matter. He was not used to them yet. His pads were clammy and stuck, and the leather was wet with dew. The long and short of it was that, try as he might, he could not get into them. He put them under his arm and, holding the sack on his shoulder, walked more soberly down to the road below. In the valley the sun was shining, and soon it turned to a hot summer's day.

Puss waited till he had passed the first hamlet, no more than a pot-house and three cottages with a farm nearby. Then he sat down by the roadside and tried to draw on his boots again. This time he was more successful. He got the left boot on, but struggle how he might, he could not manage the right-hand one. In this situation he relieved his feelings first by swearing and cursing, and then he sat silently, looking first at his paw and then at the boot. He determined that he would on no account take off the left-hand boot, and that the only thing to be done was to go forward until he met with someone willing to help him. The first person he passed was a gypsy riding a pony, but Puss did not even nod or say good morning, for he did not like the man's looks. It was the same thing with the next comer, a silly girl who stood and stared as Puss limped by. No great thinker was ever in a more contemptible predicament, and, although Puss was a stout resolute fellow, he was almost beside himself with mortification. Added to this he found himself growing footsore, and, after five or six miles he lay down on the bank beside the road and wept. He could not bring himself to ask for help; there was no help to be had, yet he was sure that he could never draw the cursed boot on by himself. All his plans were likely to miscarry for lack of a shoehorn—and what could he say to his young master?

Puss sobbed with shame when he thought he would have to return and confess his failure: Christopher would never believe in him again. At length, tired out by his long and painful walk, and exhausted by his tears, Puss laid his head on the troublesome boot and fell asleep.

It was afternoon when Puss woke up, and the first thing that he saw when he opened his eyes was the wretched boot that he had used as a pillow. In his sleep he had shifted about, and now he was staring down into the top of the leg. He caught sight then of two little things which he had not noticed before. He sat up at once, reached down and caught hold of the tags which had been turned down inside the leg. Taking hold of these and putting his claws through them, he thrust his paw in and drew the boot onto his leg, and after a hard tug or two, got it on, for he had something to hold onto.

Puss's happiness at having got his fine boot on was so extreme that for some little while he did not know what to do with himself for joy. Springing up, he began to stamp his feet on the ground, then to stride up and down and, as if that were not enough, to dance, and so cut a thousand silly capers. Every now and then he would stop short and look down at his fine red morocco boots, pulled right up his furry thighs, and cry out in a kind of ecstasy, and then he would begin to dance again. Very soon he recovered himself, and, refreshed by his sleep, he pushed forward with his stick in his paw and the sack of grouse over his shoulder. He was so happy that he never felt tired, but went on and on, all through the cool night, which was indeed the best time for walking in the heat of summer, and by dawn he came into sight of the King of Northumberland's palace.

Puss took a well-earned nap until the sun had risen high. Then, after performing his customary ablutions, he went boldly up to the door of the Palace. There was a great press of carriages at the steps, with footmen running to and fro, for the King was holding a Court that morning, and all the Lords and Ladies were arriving as Puss came to the door. The sentries were calling out to the coachmen, and in the hurly-burly it was easy for Puss to slip through the main door without being questioned. Once inside, he soon found a Lord-in-waiting, told him his business and was at once taken to the King.

Puss made a deep bow while the Lord-in-waiting announced rather unceremoniously: 'Your Majesty, here are some grouse brought by a gamekeeper who looks like a cat.'

At the word 'grouse' all the King's ill-humour vanished. 'Grouse?' said he. 'Come here, my dear fellow. You shall be richly rewarded. Let me see the birds.' Then he told an attendant to send for his Cook and the Keeper of the Privy Purse, as he wanted to speak with them. Puss took the birds out of the sack and laid them on the table before the King, who picked up one after another, holding each by the upper half of the bill and, when that bent, exclaimed: 'Splendid! Young birds and nice little plump fellows! How did you get them?'

Puss bowed again and said, waving his tail: 'My master, the Marquis of Carabas, begs Your Majesty's acceptance of these birds, which are the first that he has taken this year.'

The King immediately enquired after the Marquis, asking

why he never came to Court and saying that he hoped shortly to make his acquaintance.

Puss replied very modestly that his master was a young man who had only recently come into his estate owing to the perfidy of his guardian, and that, as soon as he had settled his affairs satisfactorily, he hoped to have the honour of presenting himself.

The Cook and the Keeper of the Privy Purse came in. The Cook gave a cry of delight on seeing the birds, and the King ordered the Keeper of the Privy Purse to give Puss a gold piece for each one of them. Then the Cook led him away to the royal kitchen, stroking the grouse greedily with his greasy fingers and talking volubly as he went.

CHAPTER FIVE

Puss learns something of importance

Puss found the royal kitchens very much to his taste: he was tired after his all-night walk and grateful for a delicious meal and for being able to enjoy a few hours of rest. He was gratified also by being treated with great respect by all the serving maids, partly because of his strange looks, but much more because of the favour be had found with His Majesty. When he looked at them with his green eyes they blushed, and when he had closed his eyes one of the boldest of them said that she liked a man with a fine crop of whiskers, and they all giggled.

The best of everything had been set before him, he had been allowed forty winks in the most comfortable chair, and when he left, everyone begged him to come back again soon with some more grouse for His Majesty, so that they should have the pleasure of his company.

The gold pieces that he brought back were very useful, for

he took a room for Christopher with Mrs Nevin in the little inn at Stannersburn, while he hunted for more grouse for the King. He wanted to keep Christopher out of the way until his plans were ripe.

The first thing was to win the favour of the King and to excite his curiosity about the Marquis of Carabas.

Puss spent most of his early mornings, and often his nights, on the moors. He would climb up in the evening, before the birds went to roost under the heather and listen to the cock birds calling to each other. Then, in the most wild, lonely and inaccessible spot he could find, Puss would turn about quietly looking at the way he had come. There was nothing in sight but ling and heather and tufts of bent grass and here and there scattered boulders and the bare outlines of the savage hills against the sky. The wild and solitary place rejoiced his heart; he felt the Wild Cat of Inverness stirring in his blood, and he sometimes wondered why he had wasted half a lifetime keeping the mill free of vermin when he might have been living a wild life of freedom. Puss had very good eyesight; he had the setting sun at his back, and he noted every movement in the heather. Often he saw a grouse, sometimes quite close, but he stayed motionless, only the tip of his tail twitched. He would wait till the first light, otherwise he might scare away all the birds on that piece of moor.

As soon as he had caught a few brace, Puss carried them to the palace and presented them on behalf of his master, the Marquis. In this way he soon got to know all the Royal servants and everything that went on about the Court. The King was never tired of singing his praises and became more and more eager to meet his master, and two of the kitchen maids were dying of love for Puss, though he never paid either of them any particular attention.

One day as he was sitting at ease before the fire in the Butler's pantry, the King's Coachman came in to have a glass of Heather Ale, which they brewed in those days, and began talking about a tour that His Majesty had decided to make with the Princess along the Roman Wall into Cumberland.

'It will knock up my horses,' the Coachman said—then he added what was not true, that he had a great mind to leave the King's service rather than go on such a terrible journey and break down such splendid horses, which would never be fit for anything after they had dragged the Royal coach up and down the hills of Cumberland and along roads that were no more than sheep tracks.

But what made him and the Butler most indignant was that the Queen had planned the tour, saying that the Princess ought to get acquainted with the whole of the Kingdom and see the world, when really what Her Majesty wanted was to have the King and the Princess out of the way during the visit of a famous French troubadour. If the Princess were in the Palace, all the songs would be sung to her, and the Queen herself would get no attention.

'However, the King is now so set on the tour that nothing would make him give it up. Not even if he were shown the poem from the Frenchman that the Queen keeps locked up with her jewels. Her maid Columbine has seen it, and she says it's a scream.'

Puss pricked up his ears at all this, and, directly the Coachman had finished his glass and gone to the stable, Puss got up, said goodbye, and then ran back to Mrs Nevin's as fast as his legs would carry him.

Christopher had not seen Puss for a week and was beginning to despair of ever seeing him again, so he embraced him warmly, and Mrs Nevin bustled out and told him that she had a bowl of fresh cream waiting in the larder for him and a couple of fat trout out of the river.

Much as Puss loved trout and cream, he told Christopher there was not a moment to be lost.

'If you wish to become a Prince, we must set out this moment. Give Mrs Nevin a guinea—we'll be back one day, and you must have some trout waiting for me then.'

'Become a Prince! Whatever do you mean? It would scare me to death to have to talk to gentlefolk,' exclaimed Christopher.

Puss laughed at him scornfully, told him to get his change from Mrs Nevin and put on his boots, for they must be on the road at once. They would have to walk all night to get there in time.

'Now listen to me,' said Mrs Nevin. 'You can take your time and have a good dinner, for there are three hill ponies in the stable, and I'll be glad to lend them to you. Martin Armstrong can go with you to bring them back. You can ride across Spade Adam's as far as Haltwhistle, and that will give you a fair start on your journey.'

This was sound sense, and Puss was glad to have his dinner of trout and cream after all. Meanwhile Martin was sent for and then busied himself in saddling the three ponies.

Now Christopher had been riding ever since he could remember, but Puss had never been astride a horse, a fact he did not care to speak of in front of Mrs Nevin. It so happened that the pony Martin gave him was the most mischievous of the three, and they had only just left the road and got out of the last field on to the moor, when his pony pretended to stumble and then shied away, and Puss went flying out of the saddle on to the turf. But that pony had made a mistake, as he soon found out. Puss was not even shaken. He sat on a stone and asked Martin to help pull off his boots. These he tied behind the saddle, and then, in one bound, was back in it again. When the pony tried to shake him off, Puss stuck in his ten claws, and however that pony bucked and twisted, Puss held firm. Very soon the piebald pony saw that Puss was his master, and after that there were no more fireworks and no more trouble.

It was dark by the time that the party had crossed Spade Adam Waste, and, as they were well ahead of the King's coach, Puss decided to spend the night at the first inn and send Martin, leading the two other ponies, back to Stannersburn on the morrow.

But before they rode into the little town, Puss reined up, untied his boots from behind the saddle and pulled them on. He needed them if he was to ask the innkeeper for lodging. The piebald pony was too tired by then to play any tricks. He had learned his lesson, and when Martin got back next day to Stannersburn he told Mrs Nevin that there was never such a jockey to ride a bucking pony as the Gentleman with Whiskers.

As soon as Christopher found himself on the road next morning alone with Puss, he said: 'I fear you would have me do something wrong. I would not do anything wrong for the world. It cannot be right that I, a miller's son, should be made a Prince. Indeed, Puss, we had better go no further.'

Puss was so angry that he sat down by the roadside and began tugging at his boots to take them off.

'What is the matter, Puss? I did not mean to make you angry. It would be better to get some more gold pieces from the King honestly than for me to forget my station in life.'

Puss tugged away at his boots and then said, spitting between each of his words: 'Once I have got these damned boots off my legs, you will never see me more. Make up your mind to that, young man.'

'Don't say that, Puss,' said Christopher. 'Don't say that. I will do anything you tell me, if you will not leave me, so long as it is nothing wrong.'

'Do you think that your father would have left me to start you in the world, if he had not trusted me?' asked Puss. 'But you are more scrupulous, or more timorous, than your father, it seems.' These words struck Christopher dumb. He began to think that he was very much in the wrong now, and that it might be filial piety in him to become a Prince. Besides he was very eager to keep Puss and to hear the whole story. One of the boots was loose and Puss was drawing it off, when Christopher said: 'Stay, Puss, and I will come with you gladly. What you say is most likely true. It may be my duty to respect my father's wishes and become a Prince. Who can tell? It may be God's will.'

'The way you talk is enough to make a cat laugh,' said Puss. 'A fine Prince you will make if you go on as you have begun.' And it would have been hard to say whether what he was saying was meant as a gibe or whether he were in earnest.

'If you go on talking in that strain you will be set down as Christopher the Good, Christopher the Righteous, or perhaps even Christopher the Meek, in all the history books.'

At these words, even though they were spoken in a peculiarly insulting and contemptuous tone of voice, Christopher began to smile with happiness and sprang up, anxious to make haste along the road and meet his destiny.

Puss pulled on the boot he had nearly got off and reflected that all Christopher's piety was now for his father, who he had been cursing ever since his death for leaving him nothing but a cat. But all was different now that he had shown himself a cat that could win a King's favour and bring home gold pieces.

As they hurried on into Cumberland, Christopher asked Puss a thousand questions as to how he was to become a Prince, but he could only get these words out of him in reply:

'You do as you are bid and all may yet go well.'

Then Puss walked faster, until Christopher was so out of breath that he could not question the cat any more.

When they had covered fifteen miles in this fashion and were come to where they could look down into the valley of the Eden, Puss called a halt and sat down in the shade of a thorn tree.

'Now there must be no more of this,' said he, still very morose. 'Before we go any further you must promise that you will do as I tell you. Otherwise it is no good hoping to be a Prince, or anything but a beggar on the roads. For that is what you will become if I go off now and leave you.'

'I promise to do everything that you tell me,' answered Christopher sulkily. 'But tell me, Puss, in what way am I to become a Prince, for I am sure that you know best what is to be done, and I am not ungrateful.'

Puss was softened by the humble way in which his young master spoke and, after twirling his whiskers in a military fashion, he replied: 'Why, I shall make you a Prince by marrying you to a Princess. You are to marry the first Princess whom we meet on the road,' and after these words Puss gave a yawn which was more than half a laugh.

Christopher blushed up to the roots of his hair, for to tell the truth he was no more than a hobbledehoy, a chawbacon, a rustic hobbinol, though he was as handsome a young man as you could find in all England and would have served the Greek sculptor Praxiteles as a model for Apollo.

When Christopher heard marriage spoken of, he was quite sure all was well. There could be nothing wrong in wedlock. And then he begged Puss's pardon over and over again for his lack of trust, and said that it had arisen because he was taken by surprise at anything so far beyond his highest hopes or deserts.

Puss soon said that they must be on the road again, and they continued downhill into the valley of the Eden, but at a more moderate pace, for Puss's right-hand boot pinched the middle claw.

CHAPTER SIX

Puss plays a cunning trick

THAT night Puss and Christopher were near their journey's end. They were tired out and ready to fall asleep
at the first inn where they could get a supper and a lodging.
Next morning Puss was up early and out for an hour before
Christopher came down to breakfast.

'All is well,' cried Puss rubbing his paws and arching his
back. 'The Princess has not passed this way yet; we need go
no further, at least not more than a mile or two to the banks of
Lake Ullswater.' By this time the miller's son had forgotten
about his station in life and quite fallen in love with the word
Princess, as well as the title Prince before the name of Christopher. There were a thousand questions he wished to ask but he
dared not, so, after paying the score at the inn for their night's
lodging and their breakfast, he had to follow Puss without saying a word.

They soon came to the lake, which has a road running

beside it with oaks and beeches by the water's edge.

Puss told his master to climb on to a rock which overlooked the road and ordered him to keep a sharp lookout for any coach that might come that way. After saying this, he settled himself very comfortably on a smooth rock in the blazing sun and went to sleep. Christopher sat above him. He soon grew tired of watching the road, but whenever he took his eyes off it, he found that Puss was watching him through his half-shut lids.

When they had been waiting three hours and Christopher was ready to drop with the heat, he saw a coach drawn by six piebald horses with three postilions in scarlet liveries, come into view about a mile off. There were footmen running before, and the sun caught the tips of the lances and the shining helmets of cavalry behind.

Christopher called out to Puss, who told him to take off all his clothes and to swim out into the lake, but to stay within earshot.

'That is what we have been waiting for,' said Puss as his master undressed. 'This is the King's coach and horses. These are the King's men, and with the King is the Princess whom you are to marry. Hide yourself in that clump of bulrushes, but come out when the coach has stopped, and mind you do not show surprise at anything or contradict anything I say. All I will tell you now is that your name is the Marquis of Carabas and that your castle and estate are not far off.'

By this time Christopher had stripped off his clothes and, diving from the edge of the rock, swam out into the lake, which is what he had been longing to do during the whole of his vigil. Puss did not trouble to look at his master swimming, though he was a very beautiful young man with a skin like the petals of a wild rose and with splendidly strong shoulders and muscles that you do not see often in a gentleman, but which Christopher had gained from hard work in the mill. Puss was busy just then in making Christopher's clothes into a bundle, in the middle of which he tied a large stone and then threw it out as far as he could into the lake. In a few moments more the coach came into sight, and Puss began to run up and down the shore of the lake, wringing his paws and crying out for help. Hearing his cries, the coachman and the postilions, who recognised him, drew up at the side of the lake, and His Majesty put his head out of the window. Puss started, as though with surprise, at seeing these friendly faces and rushed up to the King, but his agitation was so great that he forgot to show any respect. He did not bow, or address him as 'Your Majesty.' Instead of that he waved his paws and screamed out in a bloodcurdling voice, from which his anguish of mind might be judged: 'Thieves! Robbers! Scoundrels! Oh, what am I to do? Curse them! Hang them! Burn them! They have stolen my master's clothes while he was bathing and taken his gold chain and his sword with the pearl handle: Scottish thieves from over the Border. What could my master do as he was swimming in the lake? What could he do naked, but dive like a dabchick and hide in the bulrushes like a grebe? I confess I hid behind that rock myself, for they were six men, well armed and mounted on ponies, and I had no weapon but my staff.'

Then he turned towards the lake and called Christopher, who came out of the bulrushes and swam to them. When he was waist deep he stood up and stayed there, for he was too modest to scramble ashore without his clothes.

The Princess looked out of the coach over her father's shoulder. In her eyes the miller's son was like a honeycomb fresh from the hive, his skin white as the cappings of wax, his hair the colour of honey itself, and the sight of his wet body, with pearly drops of water trickling down from his shoulders to his belly, promised her more delight than a broken honeycomb dripping with the sticky sweet.

All the while that the King was talking, asking questions, giving orders and offering help, the Princess gazed at the naked young man with her childish eyes full of new greed. When she recovered from her excitement, she told herself that she was in love. At Court she had met with many gallantries, compliments and advances from suitors, but the courtiers were old, and in her eyes as ugly as so many plucked fowls. They looked at her with beady eyes, while between the wrinkles in their lean throats there were little hard lumps under the skin, or pimples as big as a bird's wattles bursting through.

Presently Christopher saw the Princess looking at him over her father's shoulders; his eyes met hers, but he lowered them respectfully and blushed, remembering that his good-for-nothing pander of a cat had told him that this was the lady whom he was to marry.

Puss had no time to observe these tender exchanges of glances; he felt sure that that part of his project which depended upon the young people would not miscarry, and all his attention was for His Majesty. The King had immediately ordered the Groom-in-waiting to unpack a spare suit of his clothes for the Marquis.

Leaving them, the coach drove on for a short distance and, while Christopher dressed, hampers were unpacked and lunch set by the side of the lake.

In a short while, Christopher, looking astonishingly handsome in a suit of the King's clothes, although they were too tight across the shoulders and far too baggy round the waist, kissed the King's hand, and then His Majesty presented him to his daughter and helped him to half a cold roast duck, without getting up from the camp stool on which he was seated.

Puss waited on his master during the meal, taking care to observe a very crestfallen air, so that His Majesty should see how much ashamed he was of his recent lack of decorum and of how he now sought to make amends for it by his present humility.

At last the good-natured monarch caught hold of Puss by the tail and said to him: 'Cheer up, old fellow. It was a sad accident, but it might have been much worse. But all's well that ends well, and I hope that your master will think that the lunch he is eating makes up for his long immersion and the loss of a suit of clothes. Marquis, take some more of this goose-liver and truffle pie. I can recommend it.'

No doubt if His Majesty had been of a different temper, and if he had diligently inquired into every particular, he would have discovered how Puss was imposing on him, for it is not to be supposed that a mere cat can make a fool of a monarch trained from his childhood to the art of government. But this King had the weakness of wishing to be popular among his subjects, which led him to apprehend, very early in life, that he must never ask them intelligent questions which they would find hard to answer. During a long and prosperous reign it had become second nature with him never to question, but always to accept what occurred, as a matter of course. His manners also, though so open and familiar, were of such ex-quisite courtesy that he would never have asked the Marquis a direct question about his private business. He knew nothing of him, it is true, but the young man's appearance was in his favour, and he had not forgotten his presents of game. Indeed the only thing that troubled His Majesty was that he could not recall having heard of his title, or seen the coat-of-arms of Carabas emblazoned by any of the Heralds of England. Think-ing of this, His Majesty glanced at the tags of Puss's boots, but there were no quarterings, no crest, no motto embossed upon them. Well, that could wait for a little.

When the third bottle of claret had been finished, His Majesty invited the Marquis to accompany himself and his daughter upon their little expedition in that part of the Kingdom.

'You will not be so ungallant as to refuse,' he said, and the Princess gave Christopher a soft glance. Seeing that Puss nodded to him, Christopher accepted joyfully. Then the King climbed into his coach and dropped off to sleep, and as the horses were not yet harnessed, Christopher and the Princess strolled along the edge of the lake and very soon found something to talk about.

Puss meanwhile joined the footmen, who were by now old friends of his, and made short work of a leg of roast capon, after which he set off along the road at a great pace, for he had plenty to do still before him that day.

For a few miles the country continued bare and rocky and there was only a fishermen's cabin sometimes to be seen on the opposite shore of the lake. But Puss travelled fast, and soon turned off into a fertile green valley. This was indeed out of the way the King had intended to go, but Puss had exchanged a few words with the coachman and had slipped one of Christopher's gold pieces, for he had kept one or two of them back, into the coachman's palm as a present from his master. They relied also on the King being a sound sleeper, besides which he had never been in that part of his Kingdom before and would not guess at once that the coachman had taken the wrong turning.

The road such as it was, now ran along the bottom of a valley crossing a stream again and again, sometimes by a stone bridge, sometimes only by a ford, and in those water-splashes Puss was more thankful than ever for the strong boots he wore, like a fisherman's waders, up to his thighs, for there was nothing he hated so much as a wetting. It was the middle of the afternoon, and in the fields on each side of the road there were haymakers who were gathering in the hay which had been lying out for a week.

'Hullo, my good people,' shouted Puss. 'The King is coming this way. He will ask whose land this is, and you must all answer: "It belongs to the Marquis of Carabas!"'

Puss looked very terrible as he said this, twirling his whiskers, lashing his tail and opening and shutting his left eye, so that when he bawled out, 'If you don't, he will have you all chopped up as small as herbs for the pot!' the poor haymakers, who did not want to quarrel with anyone, shook in their shoes and promised faithfully to do as they were bid.

Puss ran on further and came presently to a man who was building a dry stone wall round a field with some sheep in it.

'Hullo, my man,' called out Puss. 'The King is passing this way, and he will ask you whose this field is and who owns those sheep, and you must make answer: "It all belongs to the Marquis, your Majesty." Then, if he asks, "What Marquis?" you must say: "I never heard of any other Marquis. Surely you are acquainted with him, Your Majesty?"'

The mason answered this rather independently, that he might not remember the words, and would the King like to be made a fool of? So Puss smiled and beckoned to him and held out his paw with a gold piece in it.

'Thank'ee, thank'ee, master cat,' said the mason, who did not often see more than a shilling at one time, and he held out his palm and tugged at his forelock. But the next moment Puss dug his claws into the fellow's wrist, twisting it and holding it so that he could not escape.

'Now do you remember what you have to say?' asked Puss, still gripping him fast and working his claws up and down.

'Mercy, mercy,' screamed the poor mason. 'I'll not fail your worship. First I'll say: "It all belongs to the Markis," and then if he asks what Markis, I'll answer: "I never heard of but one, Your Majesty. Surely your Majesty must be acquainted with him?"'

'That's right,' answered Puss, giving him the coin, 'Keep

faith or I will come back the very first time you fall asleep and if you wake up, you will never know yourself . . .'

But Puss left his threats unfinished and ran along the valley as fast as his legs could carry him, for he thought he heard the rumble of the King's coach coming up behind.

Soon he came to a field of reapers, cutting the oats, and he called out as he had done before and told them they must say: 'It all belongs to the Marquis of Carabas!' 'And if you don't, I shall hear of it and come back in the middle of the night, and when you wake up you will none of you be able to recognise each other!'

Then he ran on at top speed to where at the end of the green valley a castle stood on a mount in a gap between the steep sides of the fells.

CHAPTER SEVEN

A Scottish Ogre described

THE Lord of this castle was a Scotsman who had conspired against the King of Scotland and fled across the Border. He was of the family of the Black Douglas and, after years of travel in Egypt and Arabia, had set himself up in England and was the owner of the vast estates through which Puss and the King of Northumberland had been travelling. He was lord of a score of manors, besides which he was the Principal Officer to all the covens of witches round about, Visiting Devil to the County of Fife in Scotland, a notable enchanter, a necromancer who gave himself up to the practice of algebra and other devilish arts which he had learnt from the Saracens. At the time we speak of he was busily refining an Elixir of Life in an alembic, and in roasting some ore from the Hebrides in which he believed there were traces of the Philosopher's Stone.

In person he was a small, near-sighted, pockmarked man, with a little dark beard flecked with grey. His dress, a rusty gown lined with weasels' skins, was threadbare and eaten into holes by aquafortis and other acids he used in his alchemist's laboratory. His fingers were much bitten with vitriol; scraps of porridge clung to his beard, and his linen was spotted with ink, for he was a great writer and wore an inkhorn at his belt and a goose quill behind his ear. Puss in Boots was well acquainted with everything that concerned this ogre, for cats are fond of gossiping together, besides which they consort with witches. They may play the innocent, but one and all are guilty of knowing something more than they should. The accusation is not only that witches have cats, for they have dogs too—black dogs—and yet dogs have never been taxed with the black art. No, every cat likes to be abroad at night, and not one of them will answer how he has spent his time. Then they are commonly found on the tops of roofs, where they could never have mounted by themselves. Dogs, even black ones, are never, or very seldom, seen on a house-top. This one point of their being found on roofs would convict cats before any jury of twelve ordinary Englishmen. For how could they get there if they were not dropped by witches? That is the charge against them: that they fly with the dark sisterhood, and, however cats may perjure themselves, it will be believed till the end of time.

Puss in Boots had no love for the Devil; he was as innocent of evil as any cat that ever lived. He had never dabbled in any mysteries, but he had heard others boast of flying with their mistresses and even calling themselves familiars of the Devil.

However, a few years before the old miller died, something came to light which quite took away the conceit of these boasters and set all the cats in Britain in an uproar, and after that there was a great coldness between the witches and the cats. The fact was this: at one of the great assemblies of witches in Scotland, on the coast of Fife, all the cats were seized on suddenly, bound paw and paw, after which the witches embarked in boats and rowed up and down the coast, even into Angus, throwing their cats into the sea, and by that means raised a tempest in which the King of Scotland's ship narrowly escaped being wrecked and many innocent sailors, less lucky than the King, were drowned. The facts came out because one of the cats chanced to be cast safe on shore as the tide was ebbing, and when he had bitten through the thongs which bound him, he got clear away. The storm that this cat raised among his fellows on land was greater than the tempest which blew at sea, and it took longer to subside. Moreover this cat revealed that the witches had drowned their familiar and trusting pussies on the orders of this same Lord Douglas to the gates of whose castle came Puss in Boots.

After the news got out, all through England and Scotland the cats met in great assemblies to denounce the witches and to eschew the Devil and all his arts, binding themselves in a covenant never to serve Him more.

At Durham a great assembly of cats broke into the Cathedral at midnight and passed in single file round the altar, each Puss bowing and taking an oath never to assist, nor to be even the passive familiar, of any witch or Devil thereafter. Three black toms that boggled over the oath were taken straightway to the crypt and there strangled. Like scenes were enacted all over Scotland and England, most particularly at Warboys in Huntingdon, a village, if I may so express myself, lousy with witches. Everywhere men remarked on the commotion, and after a week a story got about that there was a Peter the Hermit among the cats, who went about preaching to them and stirring them up to go on a crusade. To tell the truth this rumour was not altogether without foundation, but the cats durst not trust themselves to the sea, and after a little while the stir died down. The facts came to the knowledge of the Scotch King and many witches were taken up and put on trial. It was then that the Lord Douglas had to fly the Kingdom. These facts are all well known and have been attested in Scottish courts of law before Scottish judges who are famous for fairness and integrity. But as they were the innocent victims of a cruel deception, no cats were charged with raising the tempest, and there was not one of them found to turn King's evidence.

The English witches and those who escaped arrest in Scotland, missing their cats, and finding the whole tribe holding aloof from them, were much troubled by it, but they lay low, and then, secretly stealing a kitten here and there, they presently had cats among them again.

Puss in Boots had taken the oath with the others, and he knew well enough that this enchanter, the Lord Douglas, was the first to have devised the way of raising storms at sea by throwing into it cats with their paws bound. It has indeed been practised almost into our own time by wreckers in Cornwall. Such was the enchanter whom Puss had come to engage; and, without breaking his stride, without pausing to reflect, or betraying the least signs of fear, though he well knew his danger, Puss in Boots marched to the doorway and blew a blast on the horn which hung beside it.

CHAPTER EIGHT

Puss beards the Ogre

'MULAY EL MULAY, a learned doctor of the University of Cordova,' said Puss to the porter who opened a judas in the gate and asked him his name. 'I have come from Spain to see your master, whose fame is great.' Puss was admitted, and the Ogre received him as civilly as any Ogre could do. He bade him be seated in his library and offered him a glass of buttermilk and enquired in what branch of knowledge Doctor Mulay specialised.

'Let us begin,' said Puss, 'with the material and gross phenomena which astonish the vulgar, thence let us reason upon the nature of matter, from which we may pass to quantities and the laws of number and so find ourselves discussing philosophy. In that we shall find plenty on which to sharpen our claws and entertain us.'

'I doubt how far I shall be able to follow you in such a debate,' said the enchanter modestly. 'I live alone here; my knowledge is from books and a few of my own experiments, my eyesight is very poor since I contracted ophthalmia in Arabia; you will see that in theory I have grown terribly rusty. There is nobody with whom I can discuss these recondite subjects, for I see no one except a few enthusiastic young girls. I teach them what I can of the sciences, but the credulity of most young women is surprising.'

'Your protean impersonations are still spoken of with admiration in Cordova. A lecture is given every year on your theory of metamorphosis.'

The Ogre beamed with pleasure. 'I flatter myself that I can still perform a few of my old tricks,' he said and with these words he assumed the form of an elephant. Puss started back with a look of admiration. A chair and a pile of books had been knocked over. Lord Douglas immediately resumed his usual shape and began picking them up.

Although Puss's nerves had been sorely tried by what he had seen, he smiled at his host and said: 'I have often wondered when watching that trick . . .'

'So you have seen it before . . . And by whom?' exclaimed the Enchanter with annoyance.

'Oh, often and by many adepts . . . But, as I was saying, I have often wondered why we can only change into animals larger than ourselves. Inflation is easy, deflation impossible. And in musing on this, I have found the explanation—one which helps to prove the Lucretian theory of matter . . .' Lord Douglas began to interrupt, but Puss held up his paw and said: 'Sir, let me proceed. You can raise your objections, if any exist, afterwards. The reason is the indestructibility of matter. The atoms in the molecule may be arranged more loosely, but they cannot be packed tighter. Thus out of the molecules which make a man, a spongy elephant can be built up, but they cannot be packed tighter and produce, let us say a . . .'

'Do not elaborate your theory further, as I can refute it. You say it is impossible for the larger to be transformed into something smaller?'

'I grant that the Ethiopian can change himself into a leopard, and that a small woman is said on insufficient evidence to have changed into a vixen, but in each case the contraction was not very great, and I very much doubt whether there was any loss of weight. That most important point has never been ascertained, although the whole theory of matter depends upon it.'

'I have never tried the experiment of weighing myself, but I can prove your theories to be nonsensical, as I can change myself into the smallest of creatures.'

'Come, come,' said Puss laughing. 'I do not think you claim to be able to change yourself into a mouse.'

'Most certainly I do, I do claim it,' cried Lord Douglas eagerly, running about the room in search of a phial of liquid. If his eyesight had been better, perhaps he would not have hurried so fast, for, though Puss sat perfectly still hardly breathing, he could not keep the tip of his tail from twitching and the points of his claws gleamed through his fur mittens. At last his host found the bottle he wanted and, pouring a little into a saucer, he laid it on the floor.

'One cannot be too careful,' he said. 'There was a brother enchanter in the Isle of Man who changed himself into a candle flame. But he forgot to shut the window first and was blown out by a gust of wind and never seen again. He was a sad loss, poor fellow.'

Puss sat silent.

'That was why I put this liquid into a saucer on the floor, so that I can reach it when I am a wee tim'rous beastie. If I forgot that, I might find it difficult to climb on to the table. The dangers that a philosopher runs are very great—but our life has its rewards . . . Now watch carefully, Doctor Mulay and you will see that your theory of matter just falls to pieces.

We alchemists have advanced far beyond Lucretius, who was after all only an Epicurean poet . . .'

Puss still sat silent; his tail thumped gently on the floor. In the distance he thought he could hear the wheels of a coach.

'Well, I see that you cannot control your impatience to see the experiment. They say that seeing is believing, so watch me closely. Here goes . . .' and the Enchanter sipped the potion that he held in his hand. But as he swallowed, Puss sprang at the place where Lord Douglas had been standing. The transformation had taken place, but this time there was no recovery. For an instant a little tail hung from Puss's chops. In the next it vanished. The dangers of a philosopher's life are great indeed. But without waiting to moralise, Puss in Boots rushed to the Hall of the Castle crying aloud: 'Welcome your new master, the Marquis of Carabas.'

At his words a shower of bats and owls fell from the eaves and flapped away, and a legion of newts and toads hopped at full speed out of the back door. There was a blast on the horn at the doorway. Puss threw open the gate.

'Welcome, Your Majesty! Welcome to the Castle of the Marquis of Carabas!'

'Welcome,' cried the servants taking up his words. 'Welcome to our Master the Marquis of Carabas. Welcome to Your Majesty.'

'What, my Lord Marquis,' cried the King, who was in an excellent humour after his nap. 'Does this Castle belong to you? There can be nothing finer than this Court and all these stately buildings which surround it. Let me view it, if you please. 'Pon my word,' he went on, 'it's in the Moorish style, is it not?'

'That may well be', answered Puss in Boots, for Christopher knew nothing about styles in architecture except that some windmills were post mills and others tower mills, made with a rotating cap, and he would have been hard put to it to answer the King's question. 'The recent additions to the castle were built by my Lord's grandfather who had travelled much among the Moors in Spain. If you will step this way, my Master will show you an exact copy of the Court of Lions in the Alhambra. But to tell the truth there are so many ugly stories about the late Lord, that some think that he would have done better to have stayed at home—not but there is evil to be found everywhere.'

'Very true, Master Cat,' replied the King and crossed himself. At this a great bevy of bats flew out of the eaves and the machicolations of the towers, for not all the Devil's creatures had minded Puss's words.

The King and Puss walked round the castle together, and Christopher followed with the Princess, and there is little doubt that he marvelled more than she, for this was the first castle that he had been inside, whereas the Princess had been reared in one and had visited some hundreds.

Puss slipped away at the first opportunity and had a word with his friend, the King's cook. Together they surveyed the collation spread on the sideboard in the banqueting hall—part of a cold haggis, a jug of whey and some broken bits of oat-cake. Puss gave orders for the removal of these viands. Eggs there were in plenty, some Dunlop cheese and a basket of Scotch kale. The difficulty was the roast, for nothing could be seen but smoked haddocks and a pair of kippers.

But luckily Puss looked out of the window, and his eye fell on a fine young peacock and two peahens sunning themselves on the terrace. The cook ordered them to be caught, but it was not until Puss joined in the chase that the birds were secured and strangled. 'How long will it take you to pluck these birds?' asked Puss, but the cook answered that peacocks could be skinned and not plucked, and that the dinner would be ready in two hours' time. Puss rejoined the King, who had been changing his clothes and washing his hands.

'Is dinner ready?' he asked at once.

'Yes, Your Majesty,' replied Puss. 'But first I would like to show you over my master's cellar, so that you should select the wine that you prefer.'

The cellar was a vast big place, and Puss held a lantern while the King went from one wine bin to another brushing the dust off label after label, and then tasting a few drops from each of the barrels. Some of these were a surprise. There were several hogsheads of sherry, port and madeira, and one of Bucelas. But the greater number were of pure malt Highland whiskies—a spirit that the King had never tasted and which he approved. What with taking a nip here and another there, and coming back to compare the Talisker with the Tomatin and the Glenlivet with the Highland Park and both of them with the Islay whiskies, the time passed pleasantly, and the King was in his cups and Puss holding the lantern unsteadily, even though he had only breathed up the fumes, by the time the King's cook came down and asked if they would come up to dinner, or should he put the birds back to keep warm?

So they repaired to the dining-room, Puss giving His Majesty a hand up the cellar steps, and the cook following with half a dozen bottles of burgundy that the King had selected.

The nips of whisky that the King had taken put him into an excellent humour, and when the peacocks were put on the table he had plenty to tell the company.

'Peacocks,' said His Majesty, 'are a luxury first mentioned by Pliny. The first that had peacocks served up as a dish—correct me, Marquis, if I am in error—was Hortensius, that great orator, in a solemn feast which he made when he was consecrated High Priest. Before then the birds had been held sacred to Juno, as doves to Venus.' Puss in Boots was astonished by His Majesty's learning, as well he might be. The fact is that His Majesty knew all that was to be known about the food and drink of the Romans, which makes it more re-markable that he knew so little about the drinks of his enemies the Scots on the other side of the Border.

His Majesty hiccoughed and then continued:

'It was the Romans who introduced peacocks to this island nearly six hundred years ago. But unlike the Roman snail, the peacock does not survive unless he is cared for, and they almost died out on our barbarous island. But I am told that in France and Italy from the presence of a peacock you can tell that there is a great Lord not far off. Only very great Lords nowadays ever eat peacocks.'

'Indeed I never ate one before today,' said Christopher, who was feeling very ignorant. His Majesty laughed heartily and helped his host to some more of the breast. Puss kept the glasses full, and though Christopher was as little used to wine as he was to peacocks, he found it much to his taste, and every mouthful he drank increasing his boldness, he became very attentive to the Princess.

The King, observing this and seeing that his daughter res-ponded to the young man's advances and impressed by his wealth and mellowed by the feast, said suddenly at the end of the meal: 'Judging by my daughter's looks, it only depends upon you, my Lord Marquis, whether you become my son-in-law.'

Now whether he said that as a hint to the Princess that her bearing was too forward for his liking, or as a joke, or because he did favour the match, it was difficult to tell. But after saying those words he had a fit of the hiccoughs. Puss handed him a glass of water, and Christopher taking His Majesty at his word, stood up and bowed low and said it was the greatest happiness and honour that could befall him and that he was quite unworthy—but then asked the Princess point-blank if she were content to marry him. The Princess threw her arms round his neck and agreed, saying that she had never met a man she liked so much, and that on her part it was love at first sight.

When all had been ushered to their chambers, Puss stretched himself in front of the fire and purred himself to sleep.

CHAPTER NINE

Christopher, now a Marquis,
to marry the Princess

WHEN Puss awoke next morning he had his paws full.
He was in charge in a large strange Castle in which he
did not know the place for anything, and yet it was expected
that he should have been long familiar with every corner of it.
In this dilemma Puss did not try to pass it off, but directly he
was up, he freely confessed to the King's cook and the serving-
men who had accompanied His Majesty that both he and his
Master were strangers to the place, his Master having long
been kept out of his inheritance and having only just come
into it. But for the accident of the King coming that way, he
would never have dared to invite him into it until they had
their own staff of servants and had had time to set all to rights.

Now, with the time of the marriage approaching, it seemed
to him best to pack up and be back at once to the King's
Palace where the marriage could be solemnised.

But before this could be done, Puss was terribly put about to find clothes for his Master who could not go on wearing those which His Majesty had lent him when he came naked out of the lake. And it was the more difficult for Puss, because he knew nothing of tailoring and of the fashions then prevailing among the nobility.

Lord Douglas had been wearing a dirty fustian suit under his gown of acid-bitten weasels' skins, and Puss had little hope of finding any garment that his Master could wear in the Enchanter's wardrobe. Luckily in this he was mistaken, for while Christopher was still abed, the King's valet came to Puss to say that in a closet next to the King's bedchamber, there was a wardrobe full of splendid clothes, some of which the Marquis might wish to wear that day, and would Puss be pleased to return His Majesty's second best suit?

Puss asked the valet to select the clothes in which he thought the young Marquis would make the best appearance, since he himself was more of a gamekeeper than a Groom of the Chambers.

Later on, when Puss went over his day's work, he made a guess at why the Ogre's wardrobe was so well furnished. For if the Lord Douglas could change into an elephant at one time and into a mouse at another, he could with even greater ease change himself into a handsome young fellow with the features and limbs of an Apollo. And in that shape, dressed in the most sumptuous apparel, he could amuse himself by winning the heart of some proud and high-born virgin, or the young wife of a Prince or a nobleman during her husband's absence. He would woo the lady assiduously and then disappear, leaving her to repent her folly. In one case he had won the heart of a Duke's daughter, the marriage had been arranged, and the Black Douglas had left his bride at the church door. Insulted and injured, but still helplessly in love, the lovely girl's life had been ruined by the caprice of an Ogre old enough to be her grandfather. Though Puss in Boots was no moralist he knew that beautiful girls should beware of old men in whatever shape they may appear. What Puss did not guess was that this same Ogre was ashamed of such escapades, thinking them unfitting for the dignity of a learned man, and that after the seduction of a virgin, he always vowed that she should be the last.

By the time that the King was awake and breakfasted, Puss had made arrangements for their departure. As there were no coaches or carriage horses in the Enchanter's stables, Puss had given orders for a train of pack-horses to be brought by the neighbouring farmers. These were loaded with everything necessary for the Marquis's wedding, as well as a present of wine and whisky for the King's cellars. When all was packed and ready, they set off for the Royal Palace, which they reached four days later.

Their arrival was unexpected. The messenger who had been sent ahead to warn the Queen and to announce the betrothal of the Princess had fallen in with a half-dozen of the Charltons, who had stolen his pony and had threatened to drown him in a bog. However, they let him go unharmed, and he arrived bruised and covered in mire the day after His Majesty's return.

The Queen was in her parlour eating heather honey and sipping ratafia with Le Sire Monvit de Montcuq, a French troubadour who had fled from France, Normandy and Aquitaine. He had been declared an outlaw by the Courts of Love and fair game whom every nobleman in Provence, Aquitaine and Quercy was entitled and encouraged to shoot and gibbet like the crows, magpies and polecats hung up in a gamekeeper's larder. And as such corpses are exhibited as warnings to other vermin, so Le Sire Monvit de Montcuq would have been hung in chains to discourage strollers, musicians and poets. Only two or three of his verses have survived: from them he is thought to be the greatest poet of the Langue d'Oc.

The shouts of the sergeant to awaken the yeomen of the Guard, and the clashing of pikes as they ran to their places when the Royal coach had been sighted, startled Her Majesty; she slipped out of the Frenchman's arms, hastily dispatched him to the topmost chamber in the keep, while she and her maid Columbine hid his lute and his riding boots and re-arranged the cushions. Then, after wiping her face with a towel, she hurried to meet her spouse.

King Gunnar II of Northumberland hated all foreigners, beginning with his immediate neighbours the Scots, but including in an impartial odium Saxons south of the Trent, Cymbry beyond the Mersey and the Severn, the Irish over the sea, and then French, Burgundian, Spanish, Roman, Tuscan, Moor and Saracen in those distant parts of the earth which he knew only by hearsay. Norsemen, whether from Norway, Jutland or Iceland, the Shetlands, Orkneys or Faeroes, he looked upon as brothers, and were for the most part his kin.

For others he had abusive epithets and fixed ideas. The Scots were knock-kneed and dressed in haggis-bags, the Welsh were thieves, the Angles of Norfolk and Cambridge-shire dumplings or yellow-bellies. The Saxons lived and died asleep and walked with their feet splayed out, the French subsisted on frogs, the Romans were addicted to nameless vices, and the Spaniards were a squint-eyed race of bastard Moors.

The Queen was therefore anxious to conceal her visitor and was relieved to find that the King had so much to tell her about his adventures that he did not even inquire what she had been doing during his absence.

So when the Princess fell into her arms, and the King led forward Christopher and introduced him as her future son-in-law she was ready enough to kiss him on both cheeks and show delight.

In every Palace there are factions and intrigues. There are the old courtiers who stand well with the King but who fear they will lose their places under his successor; there are those who depend on the Queen's favour, who play upon her grievances and foment discord. They are always ready for a game of piquet at her table; they flatter her should she sing or play the virginals, and they never fail to drop hints that she is a sadly injured woman and that His Majesty is unfaithful. There are those who try to become the cronies of the heir-apparent and lead him into evil courses, so as to be able to blackmail him when he comes to the throne.

In the Court of Northumberland there were those of the first two kinds but few of the third: only a girl or two who had shared lessons with the Princess in music, French and deportment—but who more often had escaped with her from the schoolroom to raid the larder, climb trees, build huts of fir branches with the help of a willing shepherd boy, or tickle trout in the stream and then bake them on a hot stone beside its banks.

Luckily for Christopher the Princess was a tomboy. Without either of them guessing why, theirs was to be a happy marriage. Christopher adored his bride because she was a Princess of the Blood Royal, while Swanlauga loved him passionately, at first because of the beauty of his white body and splendid muscles, but as she got to know him, because he was a mixture of humble shyness and roughness, like that of the shepherd boy who had helped her build her huts and had been her willing thrall, and whom she had seduced when she was an imperious child of ten years old.

But though in secret she worshipped the man whom she had married, she was always suspicious of Puss in Boots. His green eyes would outstare hers; his strength and his decision were unnatural, and though she acknowledged his devotion to Christopher, she resented the fact that though her cajoleries and caresses would set him purring as though he were no more than a cat, he would arise and leave her without a word, stalking off to the kitchen or the guard room if he scented that anything were going amiss.

CHAPTER TEN

Christopher married and Puss promoted

THE King of Northumberland called himself a Christian and with good reason, for he had been baptised and held at the font by an Irish Saint. His father had abandoned the worship of Freya and Thor and had been converted by this same Saint. For a few years there had been a resident chaplain, and what with the monks on Holy Island nearby, the Kingdom had been a centre of the new religion.

But the King's cousin, Jarring the Left-handed, who was still a pagan, sailing from Norway and not having heard of the King's conversion, massacred all the monks, pulled down their beehive huts and melted down their communion plate. Although King Gunnar I sent messages to Ireland asking for a fresh supply of Christian brothers, and explaining the mistake, none had appeared during the lifetime of the King, or that of his son, King Gunnar II, the father of the Princess who now was to marry Christopher.

Their wedding had however to be a Christian ceremony as well as a time of feasting and rejoicing. Puss in Boots was Best Man, the King gave away his daughter to the Marquis of Carabas, and the service itself was conducted by an Irish fellow who had been a scullion at the monastery and who had escaped the massacre which took place while he had gone off birds' nesting on the cliffs. He had faint memories of the Mass and chanted a few Latin phrases to which he had given odd meanings.

Dressed in white linen, he sprinkled Christopher and his bride with holy water while he chanted: '*Glory in sex else is . . . Pasties to fill us . . . Dominoes and knucklebones . . . Mary a bee ate her.*'

The chapel of the Palace would not hold a tenth part of the great company drawn from all along the Border, made up of Charltons, Nevins, Armstrongs, Percies, Widderingtons, Fenwicks and many more, but they waved their bonnets and cheered as King Gunnar with the Princess Swanlauga on his arm, followed by Queen Quenilda with Christopher, led a procession round the grounds of the Palace.

In the great court an ox was being roasted whole, and while the servants ran in and out of the kitchen and prepared the feast, the company began dancing reels and hornpipes while Jock Armstrong played upon the Northumbrian bagpipes.

In between the dances Le Sire Monvit de Montcuq played airs upon his lute and sang a *chanson de geste* about the exploits of Garin, one of the twelve knights of Charlemagne. He was still scratching away at his lute when King Gunnar gave the signal for the company to pick and choose among the following dishes, for no one man could partake of them all:

Salmon, sturgeon, trout, grilled soles with cream, oysters, eels in jelly and smoked, baked hot lobster and cold lobster, crabs, shrimps, prawns and crayfish.

Roasted quails, larks, plovers, grouse, ptarmigan, pheasants and thrushes, partridges, ducks, geese and swan.

Venison collops with rowan berry sauce, venison pasties, numbles of the deer, haunch of venison with honey, wild boar with Cumberland sauce, smoked badgers' hams, jugged and roast hare, smoked deer's tongues, goose liver with plums, plover's eggs in pickle, saddle of mutton with red currant jelly, baked ham, cold ham, roast sucking pigs stuffed with buckwheat, an ox roasted whole.

These substantial dishes were followed by jellies, syllabubs, pankak's torte with cloudberry jam, apple dumplings and brandied cherries. Everyone present ate for six and drank for seven, recklessly mixing mugs of ale, horns of mead and metheglin with white wine from France, applejack from Devon, brandy from Aquitaine, prune from Quercy and schnapps from Jutland.

When the last reveller had hiccoughed himself to silence, and the sky was growing red, anyone would have thought that Puss was asleep also, for his eyes were slits, and he lay still without even a twitch of the tail. He was thinking of the difficult days ahead.

At the mill his only duty had been to catch the rats and mice, and life had been pleasant enough. He had only to flatter the milkmaid in the morning and in the evening leap onto the old miller's knees, tease tow on his thick leather breeches or waistcoat and poke him under his chinbeard with his muzzle. But here in the Palace there were scores of servants and hangers-on, each with his established rights and privileges, and it looked as though King Gunnar expected him to keep them in order. He would do well to make few changes at first.

The day after the wedding feast the Princess and Christopher set off on their honeymoon. Swanlauga was a young woman of great vitality, and she intended to hunt all day and make love all night. Thus the happy pair were accompanied by the Huntsmen and Whippers-in of the Royal Buckhounds, the Master and Whippers-in of the Palace Beagles, and, of course, the packs themselves, besides horses, grooms and stable-boys and many of the followers of each hunt. Swanlauga planned to hunt red deer along the border, wild boar in Kielder forest, and to take a look at the wild goats on Cheviot, though they were not expected to show much sport, as they frequented inaccessible crags. There would be hare-hunting with the Beagles on off days. The Princess thought it a good opportunity to get to know the northern part of the Kingdom and its inhabitants, as she and her husband would spend each night enjoying the forced hospitality of whatever castle, manor or farmhouse was nearest to where the hunt had ended.

Huntsmen, grooms and followers were all armed in case they should encounter a Scottish raiding party.

King Gunnar was glad when the bustle of the preparations for their departure was finally over and the young people were gone, for the wedding banquet had been followed by a headache and, most unusually, by indigestion. He slept fitfully most of the following night, and while he tossed and turned, he decided that great reforms must be made in the Palace and economies in the Kingdom. What if the Scottish King, or even the Black or Red Douglases, had seized upon his daughter's wedding night to invade Northumberland, or raid across the Border when all the men were dead drunk? He had set a bad example himself, so who could carry out the necessary changes? It must be Puss in Boots! King Gunnar was still in the same mind next morning, so he called his household together. They were a sorry crowd of girls, women and old men. All the vigorous and active had gone off with the Princess.

King Gunnar sat on his throne with Queen Quenilda on his left—and Puss in Boots on the right, a little way behind him.

Facing their Majesties were the elderly Officers of the Court drawn up in two ranks, wearing their tabards, with the Ladies-in-Waiting in their best dresses and the housemaids in starched aprons behind them, all standing in wonder, not knowing what was coming.

King Gunnar stood up, waved his sceptre and said: 'I confer upon this brave companion of Prince Christopher, the hereditary title of the Master Cat and I appoint him Grand Chamberlain of the Royal Palaces and demesnes, to whom all present and absent must swear obedience. MASTER CAT, I now invest you with your chain of office.' So saying, the King beckoned to Puss, who bowed low before him, while the King slung a gold chain about his neck and said: 'Arise our well-beloved and trusty Master Cat, thou art now empowered to carry out our Royal Will and institute the reforms so necessary for the safety of our Realm.'

But although the King was set upon great reforms, he had very little idea of what they should be. Therefore after the investiture when he and the Grand Chamberlain were alone together, he asked him: 'Well, Puss, and which reforms are you going to institute to begin with?'

The Master Cat had so far given no thought to the subject, but he put his paws together and answered modestly: 'I suggest that no dogs should be allowed inside the doors of the Palace. You remember, Sire, how the incessant barking, baying, whining and yelping made your head ache and kept you awake in the early hours before the Princess's departure.'

'A most excellent reform. But what about the Queen's lap-dogs?'

'How if we were to allow sick and ailing dogs inside? Her Majesty's pug-dog has some kind of lung trouble, and the little white object is covered with tumours and boils.'

King Gunnar laughed. 'Any other ideas, Grand Chamberlain?'

Puss hesitated for a moment, and then said: 'It may savour

of nepotism, but while I hold this high office I think that no cat should be put to death without a warrant signed by me, and that anyone maltreating a domestic cat, or hunting a Wild Cat, should on conviction have his right hand cut off.'

'A mild sentence,' said the King. He was amused by the nature of the first reforms. He knew that the Princess would be angry at the exclusion of dogs from the Palace, but he thought it was a good joke to play on her while she was away. It was time she settled down to more womanly pursuits than hunting three days a week now that she was married. He would point that out. 'Have the reforms drawn out on parchment, and I will have the Great Seal affixed.'

Part Two

CHAPTER ELEVEN

Wicked plots in high places

WHEN the King had put him in charge of reforms Puss in Boots, or to give him his new title, The Master Cat, knew that the monarch without intending it had made him the most hated figure in the Royal Household. He could maintain himself for a while by the King's favour and by fear, but if he were wise he would keep on his guard.

Puss put very little faith in Prince Christopher's gratitude, for he had noticed that ever since the Princess had fallen in love with him the miller's son had avoided him and had been impatient of any advice. Christopher was a vain young fellow, and the rise in his fortunes had fed his vanity. From the first he had resented having to be obedient to his father's old tom cat, and now that he found himself upon a pinnacle of good fortune he persuaded himself it was more his doing than Puss's help which had set him there. After all, it was he whom the Princess had fallen in love with at first sight, not Puss.

Christopher was also afraid of Puss, who had only to open his mouth and let out the secret of his humble origin to cause a scandal that would ruin him. Now that the old King had taken a fancy to Puss, how could Christopher feel sure that the Cat would not make some indiscreet joke which would cast suspicion on him? Then there was the puzzle about the Carabas coat-of-arms—all of Puss's making. For it was Puss who had invented the title, when he might just as well have called him by the name of some Norman Duke, or why not Canute or Hengist? Altogether Christopher would have felt happier if he could have seen the last of Puss in Boots. Then he would know that he was safe. Once, looking into Puss's honest face, he had felt a sense of shame, and later he had spoken to the Princess of his gratitude to The Master Cat. Swanlauga had looked astonished and had said: 'Gratitude? Whatever do you mean? Why should you feel gratitude? He ought to feel gratitude to you for employing him in spite of the handicap of his appearance.'

'Well, he's a loyal old fellow,' said Christopher.

'So I should hope. But that's no reason for you to use a low class word like gratitude. Princes never feel gratitude; it is an emotion restricted to the poorest, humblest people. Don't use the word again or I shall begin to suspect that you are not well-born, or that you were brought up with ideas below your station in life.'

After this Christopher was careful never to feel gratitude again.

Princess Swanlauga disliked Puss. He was a strange figure, and he reminded her that there was a mystery connected with her darling husband. The Heralds had hastily concocted a coat-of-arms for Carabas—Puss had pretended to remember that it was three millstones or on a field vert with a cat's paw as crest—but it was known that they had been unable to find one in the peerages of England, France, Italy, Scotland or Ireland. They were still at work on the Carabas family tree. It annoyed her also that Puss should have become her father's favourite.

Queen Quenilda was soon frankly Puss's enemy. But to explain this you must know something about Her Majesty's interests and favourites and how Puss came to learn about them.

There was a kitchen cat in the Queen's buttery, a morose old thing, a tortoiseshell past kitten-bearing. She spent all day by the hearth and the night in the stables, for she was still artful enough to pounce on a mouse. Seeing The Master Cat sauntering through the Palace as though it belonged to him, with his gold chain of office round his neck, she bestirred herself, for here was a Palace Chamberlain after her heart from whose consanguinity she might benefit. And he did not pass her unnoticed. He was particularly polite, getting up to open the door if she chanced to want to be let out, and he even gave orders for a special piece of fish to be put out for her every morning. Like all old Queen Cats she was spiteful and censorious, but his attentions gave him a good opinion in her eyes, and she got into the way of creeping out of the Queen's larder into the Grand Chamberlain's apartments. If she found Puss there she filled his ears with tales of the cooks stealing butter, the butler watering the spirits and the scullery maids bedding with the grooms.

In this way The Master Cat was kept informed of all that went on in the Royal Kitchens and of the Queen's tantrums with her Ladies-in-Waiting, though he never doubted but what there was another side to these stories.

Mistiwap, for that was her name, was fond also of gossiping about the past, and in this way Puss learned much about the scandals of earlier years.

After the Chaplain had died of a surfeit, Queen Quenilda had gone to the witches and had secretly met with a Scottish coven from across the Border. Mistiwap was then a young cat in her first beauty, and the Queen had chosen her for a familiar. But, luckily for her, just before the time when the witches were throwing their cats into the sea because the Enchanter Lord Douglas was planning to raise a storm at sea to drown the King of Scots, she fell ill with jaundice, and the Queen had taken an upstart black tom instead of her; it was he who had been tied paw to paw and cast overboard. Since then had come the trials of the Scottish witches, and the Queen had been afraid to meet any survivors lest the facts come to King Gunnar's ears. But every little while a Lapland witch would come over on a long flight. Mistiwap said that the Queen had never dared embark on a return visit. She had heard Her Majesty boast of having flown to Lapland, but she knew all the time that the Queen had been lying asleep beside King Gunnar.

One of the Lappish witches had brought her son to live in the Palace. He was a hunchback called Turi, and it was known that his father was not a man, but a Silky from the sea, who used to crawl out over the ice to the witch's bed. And the proof was that one morning, when there had been a fresh fall of snow in the night, the tracks of the Silky were found with the marks of his flippers as he dragged himself from the witch's hovel to the edge of the ice-bound sea. Turi had a fat body and withered legs and soft brown eyes that looked at you emptily like a sad hound. Mistiwap thought that he was recruiting a coven of witches from among the young girls in the Palace.

Turi had been standing at the back of the servants when King Gunnar had appointed Puss as Grand Chamberlain of the Palace, and as he could see nothing, one of the Queen's serving-women had picked him up like a baby and held him aloft, so that he could watch King Gunnar put the gold chain round Puss in Boots' neck and hear him create him The Master Cat.

The sight filled Turi's heart with jealous fury; he bared his dog's teeth and snarled, seeing before him a rival who enjoyed greater power than himself.

But all went peacefully for the first weeks—that is until the Princess returned from her honeymoon. Then, suddenly the Palace was filled with gralloched stags, wild boars being carried into the kitchens, baskets of grouse and blackcock, while the horns and strongly scented fleece of a wild goat were exhibited in triumph.

The voice of the Princess rose above the shouting of huntsmen and grooms and the whining and baying of hounds, which, in defiance of prohibitions, rushed from room to room, snatching here a tongue from the sideboard, and there a dish of boiled pig's trotters from the servants' dining-table. By the time the hounds had been expelled from the Palace, and the new reforms explained to Swanlauga, she was an angry woman, and when her father told her that he expected her to become more womanly, she said things that were not easily forgotten.

'So you want me to become like mother and spend my time weaving spells in order to deceive my husband? Thank God when you croak, I shall be Queen in my own right and can do as I please without consulting wise women and wizards and the bastard son of a sea monster as she does.'

'Don't dare to speak of your mother like that, you wicked girl,' exclaimed King Gunnar. It was the first time he had been angry for a dozen years, and he felt a glow of satisfaction to know that he could still be so.

'It's a waste of time telling you about Mother. None so blind as those that won't see. But what about my dogs? Are you going to abolish this Pussy cat nonsense?'

'No! I am not!' thundered King Gunnar. 'And if you go on behaving like a bitch it will apply to you! Sergeant,' he yelled banging the table with his sceptre. The Sergeant rushed in. 'Sergeant, tell the Yeomen of the Guard to clear the place of dogs immediately and see that no more are let in to the Palace.'

The quarrel recoiled upon the head of The Master Cat, although the decree against dogs proved a dead letter. Princess Swanlauga always had three or four foxhound puppies, beagles, bassets or Border terriers in her chamber and seldom was seen without a dog of some description in her arms.

Once when Puss had occasion to visit her in her apartment, he found himself surrounded by dogs. They growled, but were shy of him because, though he smelt like a cat and looked like a cat, he wore top-boots and walked upright like a man and showed no fear. They first growled and then looked anxiously at their mistress hoping for an order. But instead of giving them one, Princess Swanlauga made a mock apology.

'Sorry about all these dogs, Master Cat. But there's been a frightful outbreak of hard-pad among the young entry. It's infectious. I don't know whether you had better come in. I suppose that cats do get it? They are all in quarantine, so I'm within the letter of the law, aren't I?'

Puss bowed low.

'Let me know if you want the kennels whitewashed, or sulphur candles burned,' he said. He knew that if the Princess had called out: 'Seize him,' he would have been torn in pieces.

But Puss's assurance, and his tact in accepting her ridiculous story of hard-pad, impressed Swanlauga, and for some months longer she avoided picking a quarrel. She did not want to make things worse with her father than they were. The trouble came a few months later from another quarter.

Master Turi hatched a plot to rid the Kingdom of the accursed cat and persuaded Queen Quenilda to approve it. She had been deeply offended by Puss's words about her beloved pug-dog and the little white bitch given her by the French

Troubadour, who had left directly after the wedding for the Scottish Court.

Turi's plan was to use a Lappish witch's spell. 'A wolf, a bat's liver and the eggs and claspers of a pair of mating dogfish are needed, together with some of Master Cat's whiskers.' However, the plot involved waiting until Njal, the King's forester, had trapped a wolf and Snorrjing the fisherman had netted a pair of mating dogfish. Thus it was not until April that Queen Quenilda called in a cajoling voice to little Helga to bring her the pair of Spanish scissors.

Helga ran to fetch them and was back in time to hear Turi say to the Queen: 'I repeat that it is infallible. I grind them in a mortar, and when the wolf has swallowed the paste, Master Cat will arch his back for the last time and fall into convulsions from which he will never recover.' Then the Queen turned to Helga and said: 'Go with Turi, my child, and do what he tells you. You are very fond of dear Turi, aren't you?'

Helga had always been afraid of Turi, and she shivered when he put his cold flipper on her shoulder and pushed her in front of him to The Master Cat's room.

Puss was lying on a couch, deep in contemplation, and anyone would have thought he was asleep when little Helga stole into his room on tiptoe with the scissors hidden under her apron. She was a child of nine years old, with fair hair that hung down in two plaits to her shoulders and with bright blue eyes. Though she sometimes seemed dreamy, she was a sharp little thing, which was why the Queen had picked her out from among the other thralls' children to be trained up as one of her attendants. Now in the twilit room she stole up to The Master Cat, who seemed to know nothing of her being there in the room with him. His long whiskers were bent forward in a semi-circle before his mouth. It was all that Puss could do to stop himself from yawning.

Helga lifted the scissors, but, before she could snip, they

were knocked out of her hand, and she herself flew into the air, spinning over and over, and then was caught by the strong furry arms and sent spinning up again. Three times The Master Cat threw her into the air before he tossed her lightly into a far corner of the room. The breath had been knocked out of her, but she was more frightened than hurt, for Puss had not drawn a single drop of her blood. He let her rest until she was breathing again, then he advanced on her and tore off her little frock and her little drawers so that she was entirely naked. Helga gazed with terror at the great green eyes, and then The Master Cat licked her face and her whole body with his rough tongue.

'Poor little mouse,' he said and gave a growl that was half a laugh. Helga was still faint with fear, but The Master Cat laid her gently on the couch and then lay down beside her with his strong furry arm laid across her body. He began to purr gently only interrupting himself to say again: 'Poor little mouse.'

Seeing that he did not harm her, Helga recovered her courage enough to say: 'Sir, I am not a mouse, but a little girl and the Queen's Chambermaid.'

'Little girls and Pussycats should love one another and not hurt each other with scissors and claws. I hope you did not feel mine just now?' said Puss.

'No, I don't think I did . . . but . . .' and Helga burst into tears and then confessed that she had been told to cut off his whiskers so that Master Turi could make magic with them —a magic that would send The Master Cat into convulsions.

'But now that I have told you this I shall be beaten when I get back, and even if my life is spared, I shall be sent back to the forest to guard the sows and piglets and, like them, live on acorns.'

'I know a better way,' said Puss. 'Wait here until I come back, but you may put on your frock.' Then picking up the scissors, Puss went out and looked into the housemaid's cupboard. He examined all the brooms carefully, then took one of them and brought it back to his room. From the head of the broom he cut a bunch of bristles which he spread out on the table.

'Pick out the ones that match my whiskers best,' he said, and Helga came and held up one after another against his muzzle. At last they were both satisfied, and The Master Cat told her to take them back to Turi.

'Let's see what he can do with these,' he said and gave his yawn that was a laugh. When Helga had gone he tied up his head in a big handkerchief so that his whiskers were hidden.

To everyone who stopped and asked why his head was bandaged he complained that he had the toothache.

Turi was in high glee when Helga came back with the whiskers. He pounded up his bat's liver and the claspers and curly purse-eggs of the dogfish with the chopped-up bristles. That evening he fed the paste to the half-starved wolf, while Queen Quenilda looked on in fear and wonder. But next morning who should she see but The Master Cat strolling in the courtyard, his head unbandaged and one paw carelessly caressing his whiskers.

While she was telling Turi that his spells had gone wrong, the housemaid asked if she might speak with her on something extraordinary.

'Your Majesty, my broom has fallen to pieces in the night. It was bought only a month ago, and it was my pride and joy when I put it away yesterday . . . Could a witch have been riding it in the night? I hardly like to touch the pieces.'

The Queen guessed then what trick The Master Cat had played on Turi, and she was so angry that she took to her bed for three days. Master Turi knew that Helga must have told Puss of his plan, and the Queen dismissed her from her service meaning to poison her later. But The Master Cat took her as his own handmaid, and every night she slept in his room safe from the hunchback's vengeance. On cold nights the little girl was glad to lie close, embraced by his furry arms, and to fall asleep to the sound of his purr.

CHAPTER TWELVE

King Gunnar falls sick

DURING the first months after he was appointed His Majesty's Privy paw, the passage outside the chambers of The Master Cat was crowded with suppliants. Everyone from the King's cousin, Njal of the Silver Cups, down to the humblest scullerymaid came to make obeisance and ask a favour. And if it was one which involved The Master Cat shutting his eyes to one of the Palace bye-laws, they would offer bribes.

Like all cats Puss in Boots loved flattery, and though he despised the false fawning humility which surrounded him, he liked bribes: or rather he accepted some and rejected others.

Pieces of silver and gold he waved away with conscious virtue. But if the bribe took the form of a pot of thick cream, a piece of fresh calves' liver, or the roe of a salmon caught that morning, it was a different story. In those days of his glory The Master Cat grew very sleek and fat, and his fur glinted as though each of the hairs were tipped either with gold or bronze or jet.

But, alas, the health of good King Gunnar II was failing. Ever since the wedding feast he had been seized with bouts of the hiccoughs and although the beakers of hot malt whisky and honey that Puss in Boots prescribed gave him temporary relief, the hiccupping continually came back, and often woke him up at night. He lasted through the summer but one morning in November he had fever and was confined to his bed. He spent the day there with The Master Cat beside him, for his gentle purring and stroking the royal forehead soothed the King and induced sleep, though it were but a cat's sleep. While the King lay sick and near his end Christopher and the Princess were out all of the day hunting, or, if the snow lay too thick on the fells, they gave themselves up merrily to winter sports, tobogganing down the slopes, sliding on Laplanders' snow runners, or on a frozen tarn with deer's shinbones tied under their boots. Wherever they went they were surrounded by yapping, barking or whimpering hounds.

During the hours of daylight the Palace was silent, while the dying King lay with Puss sitting beside him. But at sunset there was an uproar of barking dogs, and the blowing of hunting horns. The Princess's and Christopher's cronies, most of whom had started life as stable boys, filled the Great Hall with shouting and boasting of the part they had played in the day's sport. Swaggering in front of the blazing fireplace, swilling mulled ale, or tossing off noggins of sloe gin and swinging their arms about their chests to restore the circulation in their numb fingers, they gave no thought to their dying sovereign. If at such a moment, Puss wearing his gold chain of office and carrying a silver stick, were to cross the hall, as like as not one of these ill-conditioned fellows would jerk his head at him and ask: 'When are we going to see you in the hunting field, Master Cat? The hounds treed a Wild Cat in the wood below the Dovestone. Would you had been there to talk with him. Of course, knowing the laws now made about the protection of cats, the master called the hounds off and left the ill-tempered beast there. Otherwise he was an easy mark with a crossbow.' Then as Puss passed quietly on his way, the fellow would whisper something to his neighbour and they would break into guffaws. It was easy for Puss to guess that he was whispering: 'If once we got the hounds on to his scent, we would have a real good day's sport.'

Often when Puss strode into the dining-hall, Christopher would look away, then start suddenly as though he had forgotten something of importance and hastily leave. The Master Cat could see that his former master was avoiding him, but it did not immediately occur to him why the miller's son who was now a Prince should do so. But the explanation was a simple one: It was Puss in Boots who had set him where he was; it was Puss in Boots alone who knew of his humble origin. He was afraid of The Master Cat, who could, if he wished, ruin him, or at least cause a great scandal. Christopher was a simple ordinary boy; it was not in his nature to feel humility. He could not read into Puss's heart and know that even if loyalty to Christopher and still more to the old miller, his first master, were not sufficient to make him keep the secret, his own pride and self-respect would keep him silent. So that when Christopher saw The Master Cat near him, or even when he thought of him, he wished that he were far away so that he himself should be safe.

Indeed, once when the Princess spoke of changes that might be made after the death of King Gunnar, Christopher said: 'I think that Northumberland should seek alliances abroad. You could not do better than to send The Master Cat to negotiate agreements with the King of France and the Emperor of the Roman Empire, or even with Prester John himself.'

The Princess, who was even more in love with Christopher after the honeymoon than the day on which she first set eyes on him, was never tempted to try and puzzle out the mystery that lay behind her husband's having had such a strange sort of servingman as Puss. She was a healthy Northumbrian girl with a shrewd sense of politics and the art of governing. She knew by instinct that mysteries are best swept under the table and that what the eye doesn't see the heart doesn't grieve over. She believed also that what was good for her was good for her people and, indeed, that whatever was good for her was good in itself. Next to her love for Christopher was her love of dogs: at the sight of a strange puppy, spaniel, whelp or hound, she threw herself on her knees to embrace the animal, crying out: 'How sweet! How sweet!'

She might have become reconciled to Puss if he had been pensioned off instead of King Gunnar having elevated him to high office. He had told her many times that he was happier to depart this life now that he could leave the affairs of the realm in such good hands as the paws of Master Cat.

'He is the only one at Court whom you can trust and who will protect you from all the dangers that hedge a crown,' he would say to her. Such blind trust in his favourite shocked the Princess, and Puss's devoted attendance at her father's sickbed seemed to prove that he was, like all his race, a flatterer and a cruel schemer, all of whose actions were dictated by ulterior motives.

One morning, when The Master Cat was busy giving orders for the day in the Royal Kitchens, Queen Quenilda took the opportunity to visit the sickroom. What passed between the King and his Queen is known to nobody, but they had not been long together before the Queen rushed to the door, threw it open and called for help.

Footmen and chambermaids came running, and it was clear to all that His Majesty was in a seizure. He was scarlet in the face, with his eyes starting out of their orbits, unable to breathe.

The Master Cat came running with the rest and took it upon himself to lift the King up in bed, to force open his mouth and pull his tongue forward and then to raise and lower his arms until breathing was again established. Thanks to these actions the King recovered from his apoplexy, but after this stroke he could no longer speak or move his right arm. The King lay paralysed and speechless, while Puss waited patiently beside him. The waiting would not be for long.

After the news of His Majesty's approaching death spread through the Palace the serving maids no longer swept and dusted but gathered to whisper in little groups, and the scullions seized upon pies in the larder, helped themselves to ale from the barrel and did not bother to knock home the spigot, or even left the tap running after the jug was full.

The Princess came twice to her father's bedside, shed tears and stayed for a minute or two, while Christopher stood by the door longing to get away. Only The Master Cat remained watching by his Royal Master, giving him sips of broth and soothing the fevered brow with gentle paw.

King Gunnar died, and his body was laid out in state: the Princess was proclaimed Queen, but before the body of the King could be buried, or she could be crowned, a shepherd boy came running to the Palace with the news that an Irish Bishop with a dozen monks and acolytes had disembarked near the mouth of the river and were on their way to the Palace.

CHAPTER THIRTEEN

Irish Missionaries arrive, and Christopher proves treacherous

THE King's charger, which was to be slaughtered and buried with him, was reprieved, and the pagan ceremonies for the burial and the plans for the coronation were halted. Master Turi's whiskers were shaved off, and, fitted out in a black cassock, he was sent off in a sledge by Queen Quenilda in secret to greet the Christians with offerings of buttermilk and barley bread and a side of smoked salmon, the traditional humble fare of the Irish hierarchy of Saints.

It was snowing with great flakes, like swans' feathers, falling thickly on everyone assembled on the steps of the Palace to greet the party of Christians as they entered the great courtyard of the Palace. The young Queen stood in the centre with Christopher on her right hand and Queen Quenilda on her left. Puss, wearing his chain of office and a new pair of boots made of green morocco, stood at Christopher's right hand.

The first to enter the courtyard was a gigantic Irishman carrying the cross.

His bare head was covered in snow and the tangled glibbe which hung down to his eyebrows was as white as his beard. Between the two was a very red nose, and sharp little grey eyes looked out with malice at the assembly. His broad shoulders were covered with a blue cloak stiff with frost and laced with snow. It flapped against his bare calves. His feet were thrust into pampooties made of bullock's hide. Behind him came two deacons in black cassocks, with blue noses and shaven crowns, who were helping Bishop MacConglinne along. He was warmly clad in so many garments that they hampered him in walking. Over them he wore a chasuble of stiff green brocade, richly embroidered with gold and silver thread, seed pearls and jet beads. On his head he wore a mitre in which snow had lodged and built up into a peak, and in his gloved hand he carried a crozier with a silver crook set with classical cameos, amethysts and garnets.

At the entrance of the courtyard the procession halted while two boy acolytes ran forward and tried to sprinkle holy water which, however, had frozen in the ewer, and, as in so many ceremonies, the will had to do for the deed.

Then the Bishop waved his crozier, the clouds parted. It stopped snowing, the sun burst forth and the ecclesiastics burst into a Gregorian chant.

At this the entire company, with one exception, fell on to its knees. The exception was Puss, for a cat cannot kneel, and The Master Cat found it impossible to appear to do so when wearing top boots. Puss therefore remained standing erect, though he bowed profoundly.

The Bishop advanced towards the kneeling company, which parted, leaving him to mount the steps, Queen Quenilda on one side with the women of her household, Queen Swanlauga and Prince Christopher upon the other, each group receiving the blessings that were showered upon them.

Then, suddenly Bishop MacConglinne caught sight of The Master Cat. The Irishman staggered back, looked again, crossed himself, and after uttering a strange cry in Erse, brought out the words: 'Envoy of Satan, avaunt! *Expulso te in nomine Patris et Filii. Expulso te!*' And, reaching towards Puss, he struck at him with his crozier. The stroke did not reach The Master Cat, but, seeing all eyes turned upon him, except those of Christopher and Queen Swanlauga who looked away and did not utter a word in his defence, but shrank back and behaved as though they had never seen his honest face before—well, in this situation, Puss bowed to his former master and then turned and walked quietly back through the crowd of footmen, scullions and kitchenmaids to his room.

King Gunnar's funeral was a Christian one. His grave was dug in consecrated ground where Bishop MacConglinne planned to build a church. The procession was led by the ecclesiastics, the coffin carried by six bearers wearing wolf-skins over their coats of mail followed. Then came the King's charger led by two stableboys, next came Queen Quenilda alone draped in black, then Queen Swanlauga with Christopher at her side, carrying a drawn sword as protector of the Realm. Then came Puss in Boots, The Master Cat, as holding the highest office in the land. He was wearing his chain of office and a pair of black calfskin boots specially made, and Helga had tied black ribands in neat bows on his forearms and his tail. After him came the Earls of the Kingdom, the King of Orkney and the Elder of the Shetland Thing.

But though The Master Cat had his proper place in the procession, he noticed that all edged away from him as he stood by the grave, and when the service was over the only person who greeted him was the King of Orkney who had only arrived just in time for the funeral. That jovial monarch came up and shook him warmly by the paw, saying that he was proud to meet him and that his fame had spread wherever the long ships sailed: to Iceland, Greenland and no doubt to Vineland far in the west, as well as through Britain, France and Spain. Puss was indeed, the King assured him, the most famous of his race and admired by all.

It may well be because the King of Orkney held him in talk all the way back to the Palace that no mischief befell Puss then and there. But as soon as the King and he had taken leave of each other with many bows and assurances of friendship and Puss had stepped through the door of his private apartments, a sack was pulled over his head, he was tripped up, shaken down into it and the mouth of the sack quickly tied up.

Now, if Puss had not been wearing top boots, it is certain that his captors would have a hard job to bundle his legs into the sack and that they would have paid dearly with deep lacerations from his claws. But in this dreadful predicament the boots, which had served him so well in gaining the estimation of mankind, proved his undoing, and a common cat would have been able to put up a better fight than the Grand Chamberlain with his golden chain of office and his new black top boots.

But no common cat would have behaved with the sense that Puss now showed. For, realising that he was trapped, he kept his temper, which is more than most men would have done. He lay there quietly, noting that he was in a new unused corn sack, tightly woven of the best hemp, and that to bite through it, if not impossible, would be the work of many hours. When they had finished tying the mouth of the sack, each of Puss's captors gave it a kick and laughed. Puss recognised the laugh of one as that of the whipper-in of the Queen's buckhounds.

In the sack it was soon hot and stuffy, and Puss needed more air. So, feeling about, he came to the seam and finding a long stitch he pulled it out with his claws and managed to bite the thread through. By pulling and biting he unpicked about half an inch of the seam—but he could do no more. However, by keeping his nose close to this little gap, he was able to get enough fresh air so that he would not stifle.

Once he was able to breathe freely, he lay still. He might, he thought, be able to sham dead. He knew that being put in the bag was the work of Queen Swanlauga—for the men who had caught him were her servants. But what of Christopher? He had turned away when the Irish Bishop had mistaken him for one of Satan's envoys. Would he come to his defence now, or not?

While Puss turned this over in his mind, he made himself as comfortable as he could. First he pulled off his gold chain of office, for it was clear that that would be no more good to him since King Gunnar's death. Then turning and twisting about, he managed to pull off his boots so that he would have his hinder claws free to use if it came to a fight.

He was lying still as death when the whipper-in and his mate came back. They each gave the sack a good kick, and though one of the blows almost dislocated his shoulder, Puss had the strength of will to utter no sound and make no movement. Then, without bothering themselves further, the men dragged the sack out of the Chancellory along a passage and into the Queen's Chambers.

'Here you are, Your Majesty. Master Cat may think himself clever, but he can't get out of that there bag. But I reckon that he has passed out.'

'How can that be?' It was Queen Swanlauga's voice.

'I've known a badger die in a bag 'cos he couldn't get enough air. But it took him two days,' said the whipper-in.

'I shan't take any chances,' said the Queen. Then she added: 'You've done a good job. You can go now, but stay within call as I may want you soon.'

Puss could hear the men go out and shut the door. Then he heard Christopher speak. He had not known he was there. Alone with the Queen the Prince said: 'Why did you send them away? We have only to weight the sack with some heavy stones and dump it in the river.'

'That would not do at all,' said the Queen. 'If Master Cat just disappeared, the rumour would go round that you had spirited him away and that you had saved his life. There is a lot of suspicion about your relations with him. You must get rid of the guilt of association. You must come clean out of this. It would be best to turn him over to the good Bishop and have him tried at the same time as the little girl. Then they could both be burned together.'

'It would never do to put him on trial. He might say the most frightful things in his defence,' said Christopher.

'I agree. Well, now we have him in this bag we must not let him out alive. Egbert seemed to think he might be dead now,' said the queen.

'I'll make sure of that,' said Christopher and Puss could hear him drawing his sword out of the scabbard.

Now Prince Christopher's sword was a Highland broadsword to which he had helped himself in Lord Douglas's castle. It was a fine weapon, the blade had been forged at Ferrara, but to suit the Scottish taste. It was made for cutting rather than for thrusting. So when Prince Christopher drove his sword into the sack it was a moment before the point pushed through the stout hemp, and, in that instant, Puss was able to slide his body a little to one side—though not far enough for him to escape. So, though the sword did not go right through Puss's body, the razor-sharp edge cut through the loose skin of his side below the shoulder and laid bare the ribs. When Christopher drew his sword out, it was all bloody, and blood ran out of the cut sack on to the Palace floor.

'That's settled him. Now we have nothing to fear. Not that

I ever did anything wrong—except in my stupidity I employed him. He was my uncle's servant.'

'One day you must tell me the whole story . . . It always seemed rather strange . . .' said the Queen.

'Well, I had better call Egbert back and get him to carry the corpse to MacConglinne with my compliments,' said Christopher.

'How stupid you are, darling,' cried the Queen, stamping her foot. 'It would never do to let the world know that you had killed The Master Cat when he was tied up in a bag! No, indeed. You only killed him because he sprang at me and you came to my defence. This is our story. I sent for The Master Cat and explained that the Bishop must have made a mistake, but that he would have to be tried, though we were sure he was innocent. And remember that I swore to him that he should have a fair trial. But then the wicked creature leapt at me, and would have torn me in pieces if you had not come to my rescue and cut him down. And remember this: you had always believed in his innocence, and it was only when he attacked me rather than be tried by the Bishop that you saw that he was sent by the Devil. We are both astounded that he could have taken you and my good father in for so long with his deceits. You are ready to do penance for your error, but you hope that by killing Satan's ambassador you have purged the sin. Now, darling, be sure that you stick to that story.'

'Dearest, I am sorry that I was so stupid. It is a good thing that you are the Queen and that I am only your consort. I should never have thought of the different way of telling the Bishop that he is dead.'

Queen Swanlauga gazed at Christopher with love in her eyes. 'You think that everyone is as honest and generous as you are yourself, darling, and that fair dealing comes naturally to all men because it does to you. Oh, if only the world could be made up of people like you, so kind and warm-hearted and good!'

Christopher blushed with pleasure at his wife's praises. He thought they were not undeserved.

The Queen continued: 'Perhaps it is a good thing that I was brought up in a Court and know by experience it is not safe to trust anyone. I know how they are all crafty, lying, treacherous and deceitful. As for that old Bishop—he would steal pennies from a blind man. No, we must not hand over Master Cat's body without a return: I shall drive a hard bargain with him.'

Christopher stared at her without understanding.

'Why should the Bishop want Puss's body?' he asked.

'Christians will pay almost any price for the relics of a Saint. The relics of a Devil should be worth their weight in gold.'

'Relics of a Devil? But Puss . . .' muttered Christopher.

'You and I know that he was just a cat, but the Bishop thinks he was a Servant of Satan,' explained the Queen.

Christopher thought that she was wonderfully clever to sell Puss for his weight in gold. He had once thought that Puss's skin was only worth a pair of gloves.

'Meanwhile drag the bag with his body into that cupboard, and I will wipe up the blood myself. The fewer people know about his being in a bag the better.'

And while the Queen was wiping up the blood and washing out all traces of it, she reflected that in order to be really safe, it would be best for Egbert and his mate to meet with a fatal accident before they started gossiping about how they had trapped Master Cat in a sack on the orders of the Queen.

CHAPTER FOURTEEN

Puss sold as a Devil

Puss lay quiet in the bag, only moving to lick the bleeding sword cut in his side. He had met cruel and hard-hearted men and boys—Christopher's brother John was one of them—but he had always believed that in the main men were kind and good, and he had expected that, even if Christopher were not actively grateful and disliked being reminded of how much he owed to his father's cat, he would have some warm feeling for old times sake.

He had been astonished when the young Prince had drawn his sword and pushed it through the bag to murder his old friend and benefactor trapped inside. But the Queen's praises of the Prince for his warm heart, his kindness and his honesty, made Puss see for the first time that there was no infamy that men would not commit in good faith believing that all their actions were noble. Puss saw then that just because he was a cat he meant nothing and was of no value. Puss had learned a lot since King Gunnar's death, and he was soon to learn more.

Lying in the cupboard and faint with loss of blood, Puss could hear the Queen call for one of her women and send her with a message to Bishop MacConglinne asking him to come to her Chamber at once upon an urgent matter. There was a long delay during which he heard the Queen walking up and down stamping her foot, then cursing the Bishop for his slowness.

The Queen's message had annoyed him. It would, MacConglinne thought, have been more fitting if the young Queen had asked permission to wait upon him. He therefore first kept the Queen's messenger waiting for half an hour, and then told her to say that though she had interrupted him in his devotions he was willing to receive Her Majesty.

Five minutes later two men in coats of mail and with drawn swords pushed their way into his room.

'We are here to escort you to the Queen's Chamber, my Lord,' said one of them. The Bishop had turned pale at the sight of the naked steel, and, in a voice that quavered, replied that he was grateful to Her Majesty for her forethought; then, setting his mitre on his head and taking up his crozier, he walked to the Queen's Chamber between the two men-at-arms.

'It is so good of you to come, Bishop. I have some urgent and weighty matters to discuss with you in private,' she explained, and then told the guards to wait outside and Christopher that she would like him to stay.

'Owing to your hasty and ill-considered action in denouncing my loyal and beloved servant, Master Cat, as an emissary of Satan, it has become impossible to keep him as my temporal and you as my spiritual adviser,' said the Queen. 'It has therefore become necessary for me to choose between you.'

'There is no room for choice between God and the Devil!' exclaimed the Bishop.

'There is however room for choice between you and Master Cat,' said the Queen, with her small mouth set tight. 'I could send you back to Ireland tomorrow, or you and your party might simply disappear. In either case your mission would have been a failure, and you yourself would soon be forgotten.'

The Bishop opened his mouth to speak, but the Queen signed for him to be silent, and continued: 'If that were my choice I should be carrying out my father's dying wish to put my trust in Master Cat, His Majesty's Privy Paw. But I should lay myself open to excommunication and be badly thought of in Christian countries. That would make little difference to us here in Northumberland. It would be an economy not to have to build a church, but to go on worshipping our old Standing Stones. I admit it is with sorrow that I should quarrel with the Church. Christianity seems to be the coming religion. It upholds the Divine Right of Kings and it keeps the common people in subordination. It has great merits, and I should regret being outside the Christian community. But it is your fault if I find myself there.'

The Bishop again attempted to speak, but the young Queen scowled at him and said: 'Let me conclude . . . Well, on the other hand I can hand The Master Cat, Lord Privy Paw, over to you for an ecclesiastical trial. That is the course I may decide upon. But I shall not hand him over without assurances from you.

'You must bless my marriage and confer upon my husband the title of Defender of the Faith. I require a promise that he shall be canonised a Saint after his death. Then you must proclaim the Divine Right of the Royal House of Northumberland to the Over-Lordship of All Britain and Ireland. Do you agree to give these assurances?'

'Let me take them one at a time,' said the Bishop. 'There are grave difficulties. In view of his notorious association with Satan's emissary, Prince Christopher would have to do penance.' Queen Swanlauga smiled, and, mistaking the nature of her smile, the Bishop said rapidly, and moistening his lips with his tongue, 'I suggest a pilgrimage to the shrine of Saint James and a year's abstinence from the marriage bed.'

'Back to Ireland then,' the Queen exclaimed. 'And I trust that you meet with no accident on the way, such as encountering the sons of Jarring the Left-handed upon the high seas.'

'Do not let us be too hasty, Your Majesty. There are difficulties. I could absolve Prince Christopher if he submits to my authority and makes full confession of past sins. But I cannot recognise your claim to be Queen of All Britain without coming in conflict with those recognised by a Persian Bishop who converted all Britain from Cornwall to the Banks of the Great Ouse, or those recognised by my countryman who converted the Cymbry.'

'That doesn't concern me,' said the Queen.

The Bishop continued: 'I am ready to recognise your Divine Right to rule All England south of the Scottish Border and north of the River Tees.'

'But my rule extends to the Swale!' exclaimed the Queen.

'You must remember, Your Majesty, that England is a heptarchy, and that the Swale runs through the middle of the King Of Mercia's domains.'

'From the Border to the Swale . . . and Ireland,' repeated the Queen.

'If I were to recognise that, the King of Mercia might be provoked into combining with the King of Scots to invade your Kingdom, and I should be deprived of my bishopric by the Primate of all Ireland. We should look a pair of fools if we both had to take refuge in Jutland,' said the Bishop stoutly. He was recovering his courage.

'Well, the Tees be it for the time being, I will send for Master Cat and tell him that though both Prince Christopher and I have complete faith in his innocence, he must stand an ecclesiastical trial in order to silence popular rumours.'

'You will not interfere with the due processes of the law?' asked the Bishop.

'No, my Lord. The suspicion is unworthy of you. I am a woman of my word, and we must learn to trust each other.'

'Well, that is settled,' said the Bishop smiling amiably. 'Master Cat and that little witch Helga will burn together.'

'I personally would burn that half-breed Laplander, Turi, with them. But I don't meddle in Church affairs,' said the Queen.

The Bishop held out his hand for her to kiss his ring, but the Queen only dropped him a curtsey and turned her back on him, and the Prince of the Church was escorted to his room, a thoughtful man.

CHAPTER FIFTEEN

Egbert strangled

Puss, no longer in boots, and feeling very little like The Master Cat, or the Lord Privy Paw, lay where the bag had been thrust into a dark cupboard in the Queen's Chamber, licking his wound which was still bleeding freely. He was weak from loss of blood which matted the fur all along his right side and which, without the Queen or Prince Christopher noticing it, had trickled under the closet door making a pool on the floor outside.

If his wound had been less, Puss might have tried to widen the hole in the sack where it had been pierced by Christopher's sword. He had not the strength. But while he lay there half fainting and with all his former faith in mankind destroyed, Puss made a singular resolution: that, because of Christopher's attempt to murder him and the Queen's lies, he would never again speak a single word to any human being.

Now it so happened that while Queen Swanlauga was

building a great fire in the hearth, in order to burn the bloody sack after she and Christopher had pulled the body of Puss out of it, the sky grew so dark that she could hardly see from one end of the Chamber to the other except for the leaping flames. Then came a great flash of lightning and at the same time a violent peal of thunder so that it seemed as though the Palace must have been struck. The Queen believed in omens, and she at once thought that the Bishop must have been in the right about Puss and that the Devil was now come to fetch his own.

A roar of rain drumming on the roof, filling the gutters, beating down and washing away everything in its path, followed the thunder, and the Queen's footmen came running into the room with torches to see that all was secure. They were followed by several of her frightened women. Then came another flash which lasted longer, for it was indeed a ball of fire which fell into the Palace courtyard and seemed to linger for a moment, lighting up every nook and cranny of the Queen's Chamber. It was then that one of the women uttered a scream, for there were bloody footprints on the floor where one of the men had stepped into the pool of Puss's blood by the closed door.

One of the guards then, without waiting for orders from the Queen, ran to the closet and opening the door, discovered the sack with its under side soaked in blood and catching hold of it, pulled it out into the room.

Prince Christopher stood mum and pale as death, not knowing what face to put on this new aspect of things, but the Queen saw at once that the story which she had concocted would never do now, and at once thought of another one to suit:—and one too that had the merit of some truth behind it.

'Egbert!' she cried. 'Seize Egbert and execute him. It was Egbert who brought that sack into my Chamber an hour ago telling me it was full of peats for the fire, and he stowed it away in the closet!'

Hearing his name, Egbert came into the room followed by his mate, wondering, and at a sign from the Queen they were seized by the guards.

'There has been treason in the Palace,' she cried. All the company crowded closer, as the Queen told one of the footmen to undo the sack.

At that moment Bishop MacConglinne, who had heard the woman's scream and the commotion and was himself frightened by the thunder, came into the room just after the triple knot fastening the sack had been cut and Puss was being pulled out by one of his hind legs. Not having his boots on and being soiled with blood, it was a moment or two before he was recognised as The Master Cat.

It was the Queen who first exclaimed: 'But it is our most faithful and loyal servant, Master Cat.'

And then Christopher, taking his cue from the Queen, called out: 'It is those traitors Egbert and his mate who have slain him and to incriminate Her Majesty, concealed the body in her Chamber. I demand their lives!'

'I order their instant execution!' exclaimed the Queen. 'They were always jealous of Master Cat and jeering at him. Strangle them!'

The Bishop meanwhile was intoning an exorcism designed to send the Devil to his home.

Egbert did not seem to understand what was happening. He stood silent, staring at the Queen. But his mate said loudly:

'Eh, Missus. T' can't do that to us. T' be a praiper bitch.'

But, in less than a minute, while Egbert was still staring, pony halters were slipped round their necks and drawn tight. Both men were strong, but they were thrown face downwards on the floor and their struggles availed them little. A heavy heel pressed the back of each neck on to the floor, and the free ends of the halters were strained over the shoulders of their executioners. They were held there for a full minute after their struggles had ended. Then the bodies were dragged out by the halters which had strangled them.

In the silence which followed one of the footmen took up the sack and shook out Puss's bloodstained boots and his gold chain of office.

Just then one of the maids noticed that Puss was still breathing and cried out that he was alive.

This caused further exclamations until the Queen held up her hand and commanded silence.

'My Lord Bishop, I hand Master Cat over to you. Care for his wound as though he were your own son. It is your duty to solve the mystery by a fair and impartial trial, to discover whether he is innocent of association with the Powers of Evil. Thank God that he lives and can be given a fair trial.'

Puss was lifted up, for he was too weak to walk, and carried to the Bishop's wing of the Palace. Then, while the Queen's maids were scrubbing the floor and washing away the bloody footprints, the Queen and Christopher went into the dining hall and ate a hearty meal.

'I ought to have guessed that those damned cats have nine lives,' said Christopher.

'It was a bad moment when we let the cat out of the bag,' said the Queen. And from that time Her Majesty's words have become a proverb.

CHAPTER SIXTEEN

Puss in chains

PENDING the building of a monastery and a cathedral, or even half a dozen beehive huts which was all the accommodation to which an Irish Bishop could reasonably aspire in his native land, he and his followers were lodged in a disused wing of the Palace. In the cellar, or dungeon, below this, into which light only filtered through a trapdoor and a crack in the outer wall, lay Puss.

His boots had not been restored to him; their soft leather sides had been cut up to make catapults by the stable boys. The White Stick which he carried while going about his duties had been stolen to make a whip handle by his old friend the Royal Coachman, and his gold chain of office hung closely guarded among the Queen's regalia.

Instead of a gold chain, Puss now had an iron collar riveted about his neck, fastened by a chain to a ring in the wall, and his hind legs were chained also. Bands of copper had been twisted tightly above his hocks with chains fastened to the same heavy iron ring, so that he could only move in a circle of three or four yards. The wound in his side had been left to itself, and as Puss licked it clean every few hours of the day it was slowly healing.

Before he had been thrust into the dungeon, Puss had been closely questioned by the Bishop, first in Latin, then in English, then in Erse and finally, through an interpreter, in Manx. But to none of the Bishop's questions would Puss make a reply, for he stuck to his resolution never to speak again in a human tongue. His silence put Bishop MacConglinne in a quandary. Puss's silence might be contumacious, in which case he ought to be punished for contempt of court, on the other hand it might be that the Devil, who had inhabited Puss's body, had already fled to Hell. In that case the Bishop's prisoner was no more able to answer the question put to him than any other tom cat. Indeed the animal might not even be able to understand them, in which case all his efforts were a waste of time.

Torture was employed to resolve the question, but without result. For although Puss was unable to suppress the most bloodcurdling yowls, they were the cries of a cat in pain and in no way human.

No man, woman, or child with a tender heart is able to read of tortures without shuddering and participating, by imagination, in the victim's agony, for torture is the most loathsome and unpardonable act that vile and degraded men can perform, and I shall not harrow the feelings of my readers with a description of the tortures inflicted upon Puss when chained and helpless. Moreover I believe that it injures men's minds to dwell on thoughts of cruelty, so I shall only say that to the end of his days there were marks upon Puss where the fur would never grow again, and that when he recovered his freedom he limped with his right hind foot, and that his muzzle, formerly a soft brown, flushed to apricot, had grown grey.

The Man of God, consecrated to serve Jesus Christ the merciful, who wielded the implements of torture, was subject afterwards to nightmares from which he would awake screaming and sweating with fear. And these were so frequent that his fellow monks refused to allow him to sleep in their dormitory, and he had to make his bed out of earshot. He had also to live much alone, for his companions disliked him and scorned him for the work which they made him do, and for which they were all equally guilty in the eyes of any honest man.

Every time that he was tortured, and sometimes during the torture itself, Puss was questioned, but in vain. Bishop Mac-Conglinne gave orders for the torture and sometimes watched it being carried out, all because he was anxious to interrogate a Devil and force him to confession, and in so doing learn about the constitution of Hell. But he believed that he should give even the Devil a fair trial.

For this reason, although he ordered these abominations, he allotted a young Irish monk to be Puss's defender in the Court. This young man, Brother Narney, had embraced Christianity in the belief that it was the religion of Love, of Pity, and of the Forgiveness of Sin. It was this young man's duty to win Puss's confidence and to bring him to confession and repentance as well as to speak for Puss in the Court, while Puss remained obstinately silent.

Brother Narney soon became impressed by Puss's dignity, and he did all he could to comfort him and win him from his reserve. However he was not allowed to give him food or drink, as the Bishop believed that, if the Devil's spirit could not be broken by hot irons, it might be weakened by fasting to the point when he would be forced to speak, and all the terrible truths of Hell would come jumbling out in delirium. But each time that Puss was brought before the Court, the

Bishop saw nothing before him but a cat: the largest cat that he had believed possible, though so thin that his bones showed through his loose skin and scorched fur. The eyes that looked into the Bishop's were cat's eyes. They held no message unless it were hatred and weary scorn, and, under their gaze, it was the Bishop's bloodshot watery grey eyes that looked away down at the backs of his withered old hands with the brown spots of age upon them, and the episcopal ring sliding loose upon one finger.

Puss looked at him without blinking, and though he was very tired, he was careful never to yawn, for he feared that the sight of his splendid white teeth would put it into the heads of his torturers to pull them out, and he hoped, if he lived, to have a use for them one day.

For the first weeks of his captivity Puss lay starving. Later Brother Narney was allowed to bring him a bowl of sour buttermilk and scrapings of burned oatmeal porridge, sent down from the monks' kitchen. Puss could not digest this meagre fare, and he grew so weak that in the end he could not stand and bear the weight of his chains. Once or twice a day, he would crawl to their extreme limit to where in a patch of the damp earth floor, he had made efforts to dig a little hole, but his paws were so weak that he could only make a pretence of covering it over afterwards.

Dogs are commonly fastened with a chain and a snaphook to a ring in their collars, and the monks had chosen a mastiff's chain to tether Puss, never guessing that The Master Cat had learned many tricks in his career. It was child's play for him to squeeze the snaphook open with his paws. It was therefore possible for him to free his head when he was so minded, but it was an altogether different matter as regards his legs.

When he was first made a prisoner he tugged at the twisted copper bands above his hocks, in spite of the weakness from his unhealed wound. He tugged in vain and soon learned that the metal would cut through his Achilles tendon before he could get the band over his hock. He grew resigned and paid little attention to them.

But the copper bands had been fastened above the joints when he had been in the habit of walking upright which had greatly strengthened and thickened the muscles of his legs. In the weeks of starvation and lack of exercise the muscles wasted, and one day, when he was at his weakest, Puss found that the bands were loose and that he could very nearly slip the twisted copper over the point of the hock, though it might mean pulling off fur and tearing the skin a little. From then onwards Puss knew that he could free himself, though he refrained, for he knew that once he had got the bands off he could never get them on again.

After this discovery Puss made it his daily exercise to work each of the bands to the point of the hock—from which he could have slipped it off. But he was always careful to slip it back. Even during the worst tortures he did not struggle to free himself, as if he had succeeded it would have made escape impossible later on.

Bishop MacConglinne had his hands full, and the ten monks who had accompanied him on his mission to Northumberland were worked hard. They had to convert and baptise the entire population, or at least all on whom they could safely lay hands. They had to marry the unmarried, bury the dead, divide the Kingdom into parishes, recruit and educate young men to become parish priests, which meant teaching them enough Latin to say the Mass, and to read and write. They had to organise their own little community, supervise the thralls given them by Queen Swanlauga, who would till their lands and reap their crops, the woodmen who would fell the timber, the quarrymen who would dig the stone, the skilled masons, carpenters, pargeters and tilers who would build their church and their monastery. There was thus urgent work for several generations and not as much time as they would have liked for the torture and interrogation of Puss and the tracking down and extirpation of witches. Such duties tended to be left for wet days and during a fine spell of weather Puss was left very much to himself, and when Brother Narney was sent on a mission to Westmorland there was nobody to give him a bowl of water and throw him a crust of barley bread.

Death was not far off, and Puss, knowing that his end was near, only regretted that he could not tell his story to other cats and warn his race what to expect if they were to serve Princes—or even humble men like a miller's son with no inheritance.

One evening after Brother Narney had been away for ten days and he had not tasted food in that time, Puss was lying curled up, not moving. He was not asleep, for he was too hungry, and his limbs were burning with pain and his nostrils filled with the disgusting smell of his own scorched fur. But he lay in the attitude of sleep, making himself as comfortable as the blisters on his body and the links of his heavy chain would allow.

Suddenly something fell on him out of the air and struck him on the nose. It was the body, still warm, of a fat, succulent mouse.

CHAPTER SEVENTEEN

A note on cats and owls

Puss seized it instantly and gobbled it down without inquiry as to where it had come from. Though it was but a mouthful, it made him feel stronger and better and more active. In spite of the taste of his scorched fur, he would wash his wounds. He had only been licking them for five minutes, when another mouse fell on his head. This time, after eating it, Puss was inquisitive enough to wonder where it had come from, but though he looked most carefully at the cobwebbed beams and boards which made the ceiling of the dungeon, he could see nothing to explain why delicious, freshly killed mice should fall from them.

No, there was no explanation until a quarter of an hour later, when, after a half-grown rat had fallen and been rapidly devoured, he heard a gentle mellow hoot from behind and above, and turning his head in that direction, Puss saw an owl perched on a ledge below the trapdoor.

There has been much dispute as to whether that owl was a White Barn Owl, or a Brown Tawny Owl; and bitter feelings have arisen among the *Strigidae*. It is true enough that Barn Owls most frequently make their homes in buildings, but everyone admits that Tawny Owls occasionally do so—and not so rarely either.

Unfortunately Puss merely spoke of his friend 'The Owl' and left it at that. Hazardous as it is to take sides in such a controversy, I here declare that in my opinion the probability is that it was a Tawny Owl. This because the record speaks of Puss being made aware of the owl by a gentle mellow hoot. As everyone knows the voice of the Tawny Owl is musical and mellow, whereas the Barn Owl well deserves its common appellation of 'Screech Owl'.

It was a piece of pure good luck for Puss that an owl, of whatever species, came to enter the cellar. For that owl had lived for several years and reared her broods of owlets in the deserted turrets, without ever looking into the cellar, or dungeon. But after the arrival of the Christians, a carpenter had been sent up to fix a beam in the turret and hang a bell, and since then its continual jangling had made sleep in the daytime impossible for her. It was that which made her look into the dungeon as a place where she might roost in peace, only to see Puss, whom she had always admired from a distance in the days of his glory, chained up and near death from maltreatment and starvation.

From that time onwards the good-hearted owl fed Puss in secret and usually by night, so that his gaolers would remain in ignorance of what it was that kept him alive.

Since then cats and owls have been happy to consort with each other and have indeed a sense of kinship.

Sometimes, as in the case of Puss, a Tom Cat will make a particular friend of a she owl; sometimes, as in the poem *The Owl and the Pussycat*, it is the owl who is groom and the pussycat who is the bride. But even where such tender relationships do not arise, cats and owls respect each other.

They will sometimes hunt together also and, in the twilight, I have several times seen my own familiar Puss, at Hilton Hall, run out onto the lawn at the sound of an owl's hoot. Bird and Puss would then combine to hunt together, Puss climbing a thick elder bush to drive out the roosting sparrows for the owl, a Tawny Owl, to strike down in flight. I admit I have known a dispute arise between them as to the fair division of their prey. But such quarrels often occur even between husband and wife, and, when I was watching, it was always Mistress Owl who had most recriminations to make.

CHAPTER EIGHTEEN

Little Helga acquitted

WHEN Helga saw the bleeding body of The Master Cat being carried off by his enemies, with Turi in his black cassock limping behind, she knew that she must escape at once, for it was The Master Cat alone who protected her from the vengeance of Turi and the ill-will of Queen Quenilda. So, without even waiting to take her clean frock from where it was hanging on the clothes-line, she ran off into the woods. Helga was the orphan daughter of a woodcutter and had been brought up by the wife of one of the King's swineherds. Her foster-mother had died, but the swineherd gave her a rough welcome, a pipkin of goat's milk and a crust of bread, and told her that she could rest for that day but, on the morrow, she must go with Tom, the swineherd's son, into the forest to gather acorns and to mind the swine, keeping them from straying into the fields where they would try to root open the long pie of turnips grown for cattle food.

So she set out each morning while it was still half dark and bitter cold, dragging a sack for the acorns and armed with a sharp pointed stick, into the oakwood. Tom was supposed to go with her, but he usually found some reason for delay. The oak leaves were crisp with frost under her feet, and the acorns she was supposed to gather frozen into the ground.

Later on, after sunrise, the herd of swine began moving about in the forest from where they had slept among the bracken, and sometimes at midday, when Helga was eating her miserable dinner of a few crusts of bread or oatcake and shreds of cheese rind helped down with some sour apples and a few hazel nuts, the old sow who led the herd started off towards the edge of the forest. By the time that Helga had got there, the pigs had attacked the pie of roots, shovelling the layer of earth that covered it aside and snatching away mouthfuls of the straw below to come at the turnips.

Helga ran at the old sow, an animal many times her size and weight, and stabbed at her with the point of her stick. She knew well enough that the sow would take no notice of blows, but she could feel the sharp point which sometimes even drew a drop of blood, or left a mark on the skin. Then the sow gave a squeal and turned sharp on Helga, opening her mouth and showing her teeth, but Helga stabbed her again behind the ear and the sow backed away. She would have charged at the little girl, knocked her down, bitten her, killed her and even eaten her, had she stood firm. But Helga danced about, this way and that, and stabbed her again and again, until at last the old sow owned herself defeated and turned back to the woods. If the child had tripped and fallen, the beast would have savaged her. Then, directly the sow turned, Helga picked up stones and threw them after the swine. When they had gone clear into the oakwood, she rearranged the straw and after stealing three turnips to eat raw herself, she kicked and pushed the earth back to cover the pie against the frost.

One evening, driven by hunger, a wild boar came to the pie alone. Him Helga could not tackle, and she ran as fast as she could to the hut, where the swineherd, who was a lazy man, roused himself from where he was sitting eating a bit of boiled bacon, and, calling his dog and taking his spear, went with Helga to the pie and drove off the boar, who faced the dog, but seeing the man coming with his big spear, scrambled up over the pie and made off. That evening Tom was beaten for not looking after the swine, and Helga was given a slice of pork cheese of which she gave Tom a bite when his father was not looking, for though he was lazy like his father, Helga was fond of him.

Tom always went with her grudgingly, for now that there was a girl to do the work, he did not see why he should not lie abed. And when he had to go, he would make off alone as soon as they were in the forest and spend his time setting snares for hares, or hunting the sleeping squirrels out of their dreys and then throwing squailers or slinging stones at them.

Helga would have spent her life in the forest and have grown into a strapping strong woman and, in all likelihood, have married Tom, if it had not been for one of the monks coming that way and finding that she had not been baptised. He took her back to the Palace, much against her will. She was waiting in the courtyard with half a dozen other children for the Bishop to christen them, when Turi in his cassock caught sight of her and called out: 'That little girl is Master Cat's familiar: she's a young witch. She slept with the Devil-Cat every night.'

Helga was led apart from the other children, shut up in a cell and told to repent of her sins. The first time that she was questioned by the Bishop, she told the truth: that is that Master Turi was a wizard and had sent her to cut off The Master Cat's whiskers, but that she had been caught and thrown into the air, but that afterwards the cat had forgiven her and had protected her against Turi. This was not what the Bishop wanted to hear. Helga was taken away, called a wicked little liar, beaten with the birch and locked up again in a cold cell without any supper. Next day she repeated her story and was beaten again. On the third day the Bishop asked her if she had not heard The Master Cat call on the Devil and had she not seen Satan himself with horns on his head and fiery eyes and a tail talking to Puss?

Helga said, No, she knew nothing of the Devil and had never seen him. But she said again that Master Turi was a wizard.

'Everyone knows that. You ask him about the Devil.'

'Take the lying little witch away,' ordered the Bishop. So it went on. But one day instead of beating her, the woman wardress told Helga that if she confessed the truth she would be given a pork chop, a jam turnover and a glass of milk and honey.

'What am I to say in order to get them?' asked Helga.

'You know well enough, that you heard Master Cat call on the Devil and you saw him appear and knew him by his fiery eyes, the horns on his head and his forked tail.'

Next morning Helga was led into Court where Puss stood in chains and did not even glance in her direction. She knew no help could come from him. The Bishop asked her again if she had ever heard Master Cat, prisoner at the bar, call upon Satan, and Helga replied that she had once, and that Satan had appeared and as she described the fiery eyes and the forked tail that was scaly like a viper's, it seemed to Helga that she had really seen him and that the story she was now telling was a true one.

'How could you be sure that he was the Devil?' asked the Bishop.

'He had horns, and he was green,' said Helga. Then she suddenly added: 'If you want the real truth about Satan, ask

Master Turi. He is the Old Queen's wizard, and everyone knows it.'

'Silence,' ordered the Bishop. Then, turning to the monk beside him, he said: 'By her evidence against Master Cat she has accused herself.' Helga was led back to her cell and when she asked for the pork chop and the jam turnover, the wardress laughed at her.

'No jam turnovers for little witches who tell lies about Master Turi and our dear Queen Mother.'

Next day she was taken back before the Bishop who told her that she had been proved by her own evidence to be in league with the Devil. He was just about to condemn her to be burned alive on St John's Day, when Brother Narney interposed with the words: 'I claim that this child may undergo ordeal by water. If she sinks she is innocent, if she swims she is guilty.'

'That test should really have been carried out before the trial began. In any case it is a very rough and ready one, however . . .'

'With all respect to your Lordship, the test might prove her innocent,' said Brother Narney.

Bishop MacConglinne rather impatiently gave his consent, and all present adjourned to the mill pool, the only piece of deep water near to the Palace.

The river which had wound so snakily down from the moors, at this point entered a short rocky gorge. There was a waterfall, and at one side of it a watermill had been built. Below it there was a deep round pool where the salmon rested on their way upstream to spawn, waiting until a spate swelled the waterfall, and then they leapt from ledge to ledge.

Helga was brought to the edge of the pool, and a monk was telling her to repent her evil way of life, when there was a surprise.

'I ask that Master Turi who is a wizard undergo the same

tests as I do. He has webbed feet,' said Helga in a clear but wavering voice.

There was laughter, then silence, and all looked at the hem of Master Turi's black cassock below which the tip of a pampootie was visible.

'Take off those pampooties and pull up your skirts, Friar,' ordered the Bishop. True enough, Master Turi had long black skinny toes bound together by folds of dark skin like a bat's wings. There was a gasp of astonishment and a buzz of talk.

The Bishop raised his hand and silence fell. Turi looked about him and saw faces which had suddenly grown cruel and hostile. The giant who had carried the crucifix and had planted it in the green bank beside the waterfall, rolled up his sleeves and took a step towards him.

'Master Turi shall lead the way,' declared the Bishop. Turi waited no longer, but leapt into the pool fifteen feet below, falling in a perfect dive which hardly threw up any water. He had disappeared from sight, and everyone watched, aghast and eager. Suddenly the folds of the black cassock rose to the surface, but it was not till more than a minute later that Turi's head appeared on the far side of the pool. He was swimming strongly with the surging power of his father, the Silky, and was making straight for where the river dashed in a torrent of green water out of the pool and flung itself in foam and spray from rock to rock. Then, to the astonishment of all he was seen swimming, or sliding, down the torrent which poured itself into the gorge. Any human creature would have been dashed against the rocks and battered to death, but the son of the Silky slipped past and over them, appearing and disappearing until at a bend in the gorge he vanished from their sight. Nor was Turi ever seen again by a Christian eye. For, though a great many of those assembled ran across to where the river emerged from the gorge half a mile away, to try and see whether he had reached the lower reaches of the river alive, they were too late and saw nothing.

It was therefore in front of a much smaller group that Helga underwent her ordeal. She was picked up bodily by the huge Irishman and thrown out, falling with a great splash into the pool. She disappeared at once from sight, though there was a disturbance below the surface of the water. Then the ripples died away. A quarter of an hour later the body of the drowned child was seen: a pale shape below the surface on the far side of the pool. Later that evening it was fished out with a long boathook to be carried to the church and given Christian burial. She had passed the test in spite of her association with Master Cat, and was proved not to have been a witch.

Brother Narney was exultant.

CHAPTER NINETEEN

Puss to be burned alive

Puss had exasperated Bishop MacConglinne not only by
his silence, that is by not uttering a word of human
speech, but also by his assuming falsely, or so the Bishop
believed, the manners and habits of a mere cat: yowling when
in pain, miowling when hungry and appearing not to care to
listen to or to understand the questions put to him at his trial.
It became clear to the Bishop that the Devil, or Devilkin, who
had inhabited the cat's body had either departed from it, or
was lying very low. There was no hope any longer of forcing
Puss to an open or a complete confession, and the Bishop re-
solved to be done with him.

Helga's evidence, apart from anything else, was enough to
convict the cat of association with Satan, though the child
herself had been proved innocent. He was guilty even if he
were not, as his past history indicated, a minor Devil himself.
The Bishop therefore had Puss brought before him a last time

and condemned him to be burnt at the stake on St John's eve, a sentence which was received with absolute indifference by the criminal himself.

Great preparations were made for the occasion. The site chosen was nearly a mile from the Palace on a flat stretch of ground where the grooms exercised the Queen's horses, and where races were run twice a year.

A semi-circle of wooden benches was erected for the gentry, with raised thrones for Queen Swanlauga, Prince Christopher and the Bishop. A central post was driven firmly into the ground, and a pile of faggots arranged round it, with logs above so that the pyre should take some time to be consumed.

At the appointed hour the spectators took their places. The Queen and Prince Christopher trotted up, dismounted and gave the reins of their ponies to a groom to hold and then took their seats. The Queen Mother did not attend: she had taken to her bed after the exposure and escape of her favourite, Master Turi, and her own position was none too secure.

Singing was heard, and the Bishop, wearing his mitre and his green chasuble, led a procession of monks, choirboys in white linen surplices and acolytes and youths under training for the priesthood on to the field and around the pyre. They were followed by the gigantic Irishman leading Puss in chains. Two men-at-arms carrying long-handled bills marched behind in case of trouble. But there was none, for Puss trotted along, though weakly as if he might fall, on all fours, with complete calm, seeming to be unaware that the crowd had assembled to see him being roasted alive.

He showed no resistance either while he was led and pulled up a ladder on to the pyre, pulled upright on to his hind legs and fastened to the central post, at the top of which a pair of his old boots had been nailed. He was fastened first by the chain attached to the collar about his neck and then by the chains to his hind legs, which were wound round the post in opposite directions and then knotted together. The monk who had fastened him came down the ladder, which was taken away.

A pause followed, while the monk made his way among the seated gentry to Prince Christopher's throne and asked him a question. The Queen could be seen smiling and nodding her approbation. The Prince then left his seat and followed the monk to the base of the pyre, where the monk, who had conducted the tortures, blew with a bellows on some hot embers in a pail and Prince Christopher lit the torch which had been given him. He then bent down and set light to the base of the pyre. Immediately four little boys, who had been waiting, lit the torches they carried and raced round the pyre so that it could be set alight on all four sides. Prince Christopher regained his seat amid smiles and plaudits from those nearest him.

The flames were seen to have taken hold and to be mounting up the sides, when, to the excitement of the beholders, Puss who had remained passive while the bonfire was lighted, suddenly became active, first freeing his front paws, and then apparently freed himself from the chain about his neck. At all events he bent down, doubled up on the top of the pyre. None of the spectators could see that he was working hard, pulling first one and then the other of the copper bands over the points of his hocks. By the time he had freed his legs, Puss was half strangled, or nearly suffocated by smoke. But he suddenly straightened up and choosing his path where the advancing flames were fewest, he leapt down the side of the blazing pyre. Then, scorched and scattering sparks, and holding a blazing stick between his teeth, he dashed at the young groom holding the Royal ponies, thrust the burning stick into the boy's face and leapt upon the Queen's high-mettled little mare which, with Puss digging in his claws like spurs, set off at a gallop.

Puss had made his escape down the far side of the pile of

faggots and logs which had been lit last by one of the little boys, and where the fire had not got so strong a hold. The result was that only the lowest class of people among the spectators saw his escape. They were thralls and their women, dulled by hard work and squalling unwashed children, brutalised by the bailiffs and wood-reeves who set them their stints and ordered the lash if they fell short.

The poorest class of people are always suspicious of their rulers. The cynic's voice is their consolation and the one to which they listen and give credit. For this reason many who saw Puss leap down to safety assumed that it had all been arranged in advance. They guessed that the burning of Master Cat—one of their rulers, who must have a fortune put away with which to bribe—that his condemnation and burning was all part of a show put on by that Irish Bishop to take in the Queen and perhaps the strange boy whom she had married, and who owed more to Puss than he could afford to acknowledge. The sudden execution of Egbert and his mate showed that there was something the Queen wanted to cover up. Puss's escape was a sequel.

With such thoughts in their minds, they stood stock still, winked at each other, or even dared to laugh. But not one of them was rash enough to raise an alarm which might not be welcome to their rulers on the other side of the blazing mountain of faggots.

But there, where the upper classes were ranged, the flames and smoke had already made it impossible to distinguish the post to which Puss had been chained, and it was natural for them to assume that he had collapsed on the top of the pyre.

'Bad showmanship,' one or two of the knowing men whispered to their ladies. 'Master Cat ought to have been fastened to a gallows which would have held him high enough for us to see him wriggle and burn.'

The Queen, Prince Christopher and the Bishop remained

seated on their thrones gazing at the burning pyre with a pleased expression on their faces, though they were disappointed at not seeing more.

Only a few people on their far left had caught a glimpse of the incredible spectacle of a cat-like shape, crouched in the saddle of the Queen's mare, disappearing at a gallop. The violent crackling of the fire and the roar of the flames prevented the sound of the horse's hoofs being audible. As for the groom, when he had dodged the burning brand that Puss pushed into his face, he caught hold of the bridle of the Prince's mount, swung himself into the saddle and rode off after Puss. He did not indeed hope to catch him, still less did he imagine that he could arrest him, but he knew that by the pursuit he would avoid immediate punishment, and he might be able to represent it as an act of devotion to Her Majesty.

'The heat of the fire is unendurable. Have we got to be roasted to satisfy the vanity of that old Irishman? We've done our duty and now we can go for a little ride together in the cool of the evening,' said the Queen. But as they rose to leave, the news suddenly spread that The Master Cat had escaped.

'But it's impossible,' muttered Christopher turning pale.

'What absolute nonsense,' exclaimed the Queen.

But the bearers of the bad news had seen Puss leap on to Her Majesty's mare and the groom gallop off after him. And, sure enough, the horses were gone. Her Majesty lost her temper: she was furious and screamed with rage. Naturally enough her fury was discharged at the head of the Bishop and his ecclesiastics who had been responsible for the arrangements. And if the very poorest in the Kingdom are always suspicious of their rulers, how much more reason has the supreme ruler to be suspicious? So that at once the thought struck the Queen that the Bishop could not have been so incompetent. He must have been secretly in league either with Puss, or with his Master, the Devil. And, in front of everyone,

Queen Swanlauga shouted at the Bishop that he and all his people were to leave the wing of the Palace they occupied that very night, or she would have them all thrown out neck and crop. And that she would write a letter to the Pope in Rome to accuse him of being in league with Satan.

The Queen could not actually carry out the last threat, for there was no one in the Palace who could write a letter in Latin once the Bishop and his monks were gone. But she did expel the ecclesiastics from the Palace, and Bishop Mac-Conglinne only regained her favour a year later when he instituted the abominable custom of burning a basketful of cats alive on St John's eve. This barbarity continued for many centuries. A wicker effigy of the Pope filled with live cats was burned after Queen Elizabeth's coronation. This abomination spread to France, where it was practised in the heart of Paris, until, as a boy, the good King Louis the Thirteenth begged his father to put an end to it, for he loved cats. His son, Louis the Fourteenth, revived the custom and, wearing a crown of roses, himself set fire to a bonfire of cats on the Place de la Grève. Soon afterwards the practice was given up, not because men had kinder hearts, or loved cats more, but because they no longer believed in witches.

Bishop MacConglinne, who began it, reasoned thus: 'Witches have cats as their familiars, often given them by the Devil himself. And witches can turn themselves into cats. If only one in a hundred is a witch, I am justified in burning the other ninety-nine, who are only cats after all.'

The Bishop's action led to great indignation, not only among people who loved their cats—they were too much afraid of being accused of witchcraft and being burned along with gray-malkin to protest, but among corn-merchants, millers and farmers whose granaries and sacks of corn were ravaged by rats and mice, unless defended by their cats. The corn-merchants of Northumberland petitioned the Queen saying that the cat is 'a harmless, necessary animal'—but in vain. It was this that led our greatest poet, William Shakespeare, to use the same words 'harmless and necessary' for a cat, because even in his day, believers in witchcraft were still eager to kill and to persecute their race.

But as St John's eve approached, sensible people shut up their pussies and stopped them roaming, lest they should be stolen and fall into the hands of zealous Christians.

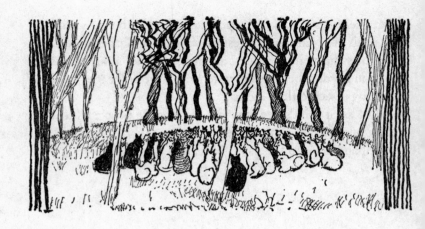

CHAPTER TWENTY

Later history and legends

PUSS IN BOOTS, as I will continue to call him, though he
never pulled on a boot again, rode to the west and soon
saw the outline of Cheviot rising above the level of the forest.
The mare's gallop had slackened to a trot, when her rider saw
that he was not pursued, and then to a walk; and when they
reached High Bleak Hope, Puss pulled up and dismounted. He
tied up the reins so that the mare should not catch her feet in
them and stumble, and patted her on the nose, to which she
responded by a snort, for she had not forgotten the shock of
feeling his ten claws driven into her flank, but they parted
amicably.

Puss in Boots was now a Free Cat, owning no master,
burdened with no duties except that which he imposed upon
himself to tell his story and to let the cats in all the countries
of the world know how he had been served, so as to let what
had happened to him be a warning to the race of cats forever.

There were no cats in the valley above High Bleak Hope running up to Cheviot. But its bracken clad sides held hares and grouse and woodcock, and Puss in Boots rested there for three weeks while he recovered his strength and grew his whiskers, which had been burned off. He knew that just as he had needed boots to impress mankind, he would not be respected by his own race if he had no whiskers.

The escape of The Master Cat gave Queen Swanlauga cause to repent having so hastily strangled Egbert and his mate, the whippers-in of the Royal Hounds. The Huntsman was nothing like so clever, and long before trackers had found that The Master Cat had ridden towards Cheviot, the scent was cold. If Puss had escaped on foot, the hounds would have been on his track very soon.

When Puss felt that he could make a respectable appearance, he travelled north up into Scotland, where his enemies in Northumberland dared not follow. Then down through Westmorland, all over the Heptarchy and into Wales, and wherever he went he told his story and spread his message. Many of the cats who listened called him their King, though they are a free people who pay no tribute and will never follow a King or a Commander to the wars.

No, the title of King of the Cats was only an honour, or mark of respect, that his race paid him. Here are some of the words in which Puss warned his race against mankind, as near as they have been handed down.

'One of the stories with which men amuse each other is of a clever monkey who induced a cat to rake hot chestnuts out of the fire, chestnuts that the monkey ate, but which the cat did not. And men say of anyone as stupid as that cat, who is made to do dangerous work of no advantage to himself that he is being used "as a cat's paw". I don't believe that a monkey has ever treated a cat in this way, but men have done so, and the cats have been as ill rewarded as in the fable. I have come here to tell you that there must be no more cats used as "cat's paws" by men.

'Those of you who enjoy being fondled and petted and having a blue riband tied about your necks, who love saucers of cream, and choice pieces of fish or liver, who like looking into the heart of a fire, or lying on a cushion in front of it, those who would rather sharpen their claws on rich brocade, than on the bark of a forest tree: all such have a right to enjoy your luxuries and indulge your pleasures at man's expense. Others of us are hardier and would rather sleep in the granary, or the barn, preying on the rats and mice, or slipping off into the game preserves to poach a hare or a partridge or a pheasant chick, as I do myself. But whichever kind of cat you may be, you must never bind yourself to a master, you must never take an oath of fidelity. Never make the least promise to man. Remember always that he is your inferior: inferior in beauty and in bodily skill, as well as in philosophy and wisdom. You may if you choose, treat him as an equal, you may even love him, for some men and women are lovable. But you must never let yourself be carried away by love or gratitude, or greediness or love of admiration, to look upon him as a superior being. You must never serve one of the human race. Look at the rusty iron collar about my neck, look at the scars upon my body. I bear these not because I did not serve man faithfully, but because I served him too well, and after I had set him upon a throne, he wished to be rid of me and thrust his sword through my side, not in fair fight, but after he had me tied up in a bag.

'You must never surrender your wild nature. Even in man's cities you can climb his tallest buildings and upon their roofs hunt pigeons and sparrows and live as free as our wild cousins in the Grampians, who hunt the capercaillie and the roe deer. Let every mother cat tell her kittens the story of Puss in Boots, who was called "The Master Cat" and "Lord Privy Paw" and wore a gold chain of office, only to be betrayed by his master and mistaken for the Devil by a crazy Irish Christian, one of those Christians who come with the message that God is Love —a message which was begun by the torture of the man who preached it. And even he believed in Devils.'

Such was the gospel that the King of the Cats preached to his race, and the grizzled old figure with a limp and the marks where the monks had seared him with red-hot irons to try and make him confess their own ugly imaginings, took ship to France and marched slowly from country to country, telling his story and giving his warning.

Everywhere cats came together to welcome him, and after his visit looked with a different eye upon the men and women in whose houses it suited them to live. Only rarely did a human hear of Puss in Boots and his progress through their lands. A legend exists that once a woodcutter, walking home over the soft pine-needles in the Black Forest, saw through the trees a circle of more than a hundred cats sitting on their tails and quietly conversing, and he heard the one nearest to him say to a latecomer taking his seat next to him; 'The King is coming tonight; he must have been a little delayed.'

The woodcutter stole away quietly, as he was scared by seeing so many cats together and having inadvertently learned their secret, and he was still more frightened when, on getting home and unlocking the door, he saw his own pussycat who had been locked up inside with no way of getting out. She looked at him intently and said: 'I'm to meet the King of the Cats tonight,' and dashed past him into the forest. Nor, the story says, did that woodcutter ever see his cat again.

Puss in Boots is known to have visited Spain and Italy and Austria and was last heard of in Poland, where he is said to have been killed, as he was standing upright against a pine tree sharpening his claws, by a bear hunter who mistook him for a bear cub. But that also is a legend, and those who tell it will not swear to it.

Puss in Boots, The Master Cat, Lord Privy Paw, has been dead for a thousand years, but he is not forgotten. Children learn the first part of the story from books of fairy tales and kittens the whole history from their mothers. But the second half is written here for the first time. I heard an outline of it from a coarse kitchen cat, as I have recorded elsewhere. Later I picked up stray bits from different Pussies in my native country of England. When I had put them together, I read the whole to my cat Tiber, in France. He made some minor corrections and when I had read it over to him a second time he agreed to certify it as the tradition of his race, and believed by him to be true in all particulars, and he has set his mark upon the page as proof.

TIBER HIS MARK

NOTE TO THE READER

EVEN apart from its magical elements, the foregoing history cannot be accepted as true in its entirety, for any schoolboy can point out that several passages contradict each other, particularly in matters of chronology. Thus everyone knows that Dick Whittington lived many centuries after the Kingdom of Northumberland was incorporated into the Kingdom of England. Again the raising of a storm at sea, supposedly by the witches on the East Coast of Scotland, took place in the early years of King James VI of Scotland, James I of England. The details of this are fully given by Dr Margaret Murray in *Witchcraft in Western Europe*. I have however, with some hesitation, preserved these absurdities, because had I attempted to remove all the incredible elements of the story, I should have had to sacrifice the *ipsissima verba* of many Pussies. And indeed it would have been difficult to know where to stop and how much would have remained.

This book has only been possible because I have been fortunate enough to collect the differing versions of many informants. The result is an authentic piece of feline folklore.

But the reader should remember that folktales almost always have a basis of fact. If we are to believe that this story has been handed down from mother cat to kittens through many hundreds of generations, it is only natural that accretions, contradictions and chronological absurdities should have crept in. What has amazed me is to have found many details of the story to be substantially the same in England and in France, or to be precise, in that part of France where I live.

I regret that, owing to my linguistic limitations, I have not been able to study the story in Italy, Spain or Germany.

It has taken me forty-seven years to collect the material now published here—forty-seven years since the first brutalised version was told me by Tabs.[1] No doubt it might have been done in less time if I had not had Siamese Cats as my companions for many years. They had never heard of Puss in Boots, who is a West European feline folk-hero.

Did he ever actually exist? The same question is asked of King Arthur and even of Robin Hood. In a few hundred years time it will be asked of Lawrence of Arabia.

But even those readers who doubt whether Puss in Boots could ever have existed will be forced to admit that the universal belief in him at the present date explains much in domestic cat psychology.

Finally I have to thank the many informants, who prefer to remain anonymous, for their trust and confidence in me and above all, my present companion, Tiber.

DAVID GARNETT

26 January 1974
Le Verger de Charry

---

[1] See *Purl and Plain* (Macmillan, 1973) p. 68.